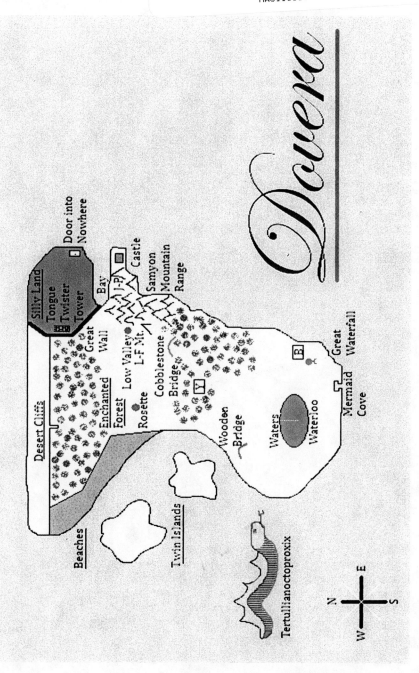

Dovera

The Morning Star

G. Davidson

authorHOUSE®

AuthorHouse™
1663 Liberty Drive
Bloomington, IN 47403
www.authorhouse.com
Phone: 1-800-839-8640

First published by AuthorHouse 1/5/2010

ISBN: 978-1-4490-6612-3 (e)
ISBN: 978-1-4490-6610-9 (sc)
ISBN: 978-1-4490-6611-6 (hc)

Library of Congress Control Number: 2009913954

Printed in the United States of America
Bloomington, Indiana

This book is printed on acid-free paper.

Dedication:

I dedicate this story to Breanne, Mom and Dad, and my little brother Christopher, who tolerated all the time I spent on their computers and gave me constant feedback about what they liked. You guys must be tired of the story by now, but know that it was all worth it now that it's complete.

In real life, my brother is two years younger and my parents are divorced; Breanne is indeed my best friend, but it's nice to put your imagination at work to see things that could only happen in make-believe.

To Mr Young

All things are possible to
him who believes
                    Mark 9:23

I hope you and your daughter
enjoy the book!

Davidson

Table of Contents

Prologue

Proverbs 22:6 (NIV)

"Train a child in the way he should go, and when he is old he will not turn from it."

When I was just a little girl, maybe one year old, my parents invented a huge metal piece of equipment that was supposed to squish and mash all the animals of the world together to make a new species, which was only referred to as 'the beast'. I was little and just learning to crawl, so I decided to try it out in their laboratory. I just so happened to crawl into their machine and it started with me inside. I got squished in with the entire natural world. They don't exactly smell like coconut perfume, you know. It's rather an occurrence; though I wouldn't recommend it. I was petrified. I was banging on the glass and crying for an hour before my mother spotted me. All the animals had vanished. They had the crazed idea that it was just a malfunction in the programming. They checked everything and it all seemed to be in order so they figured it just might not be working at all. They then wrecked it and went back to the drawing board. I think they scrapped the whole idea of making an all-in-one animal. But, being a scientist and an inventor, they would always start a new project.

I went on existing, completely unnoticed, until I was four years old. That was when I started to transform into out of the ordinary things. Well, at least that's when I remember turning into animals, I could have done it before and forgot.

When I turned four years old, we got our first little puppy, a brown Bichon Shih-Tzu female. It was the first animal I'd ever seen up close so I started to copy it. My parents were astounded at how excellent I could imitate the dog. My tongue was moving just like Coco's and I was in the right position and everything. Then, right before their eyes for ten seconds they imagined that I was the dog. They saw my ears and nose blur then appear as Coco's, until they couldn't tell me from the dog. Well at least they had the notion they imagined it because it was too extreme to be true, but it was. After that I knew I could transform into animals. Each day I would try turning into a rarer and more extreme animal. My favourites are sparrow (I can fly), monkey (I can climb), lion (I scare the wits out of people), and elephant (I'm heavy and I get a cool trunk). I also change into dog a lot so I can keep my pup company and play with her in doggy ways. My favourite game was tug-o-war. We'd grab a rope and pull each other around the yard. It was so much fun and it helped to strengthen my teeth. I also have a horrible habit of biting my nails.

୧୨

Four or five years later my parents took away my red hot-wheels race car. I was six at the time, I think. It was the first day of spring. My parents scolded me for crashing it against the wall and put on the summit of the fridge where they thought I couldn't reach it (isn't that where all parents put confiscated toys?). I had just seen a documentary on the big tall giraffe on animal planet (my favourite TV channel) and contemplated that if I was as tall as one I could reach my poor little car. I decided to try it out. I thought of the giraffe on TV and stretched my neck up. I felt a tickle in my spine, like pins-and-needles; It went all the way up my back to my neck and sent shivers to my head. I opened my little eyes to see the top of the refrigerator. I dared not to breathe for it was so dusty, but my long hair fell in my face. I blew: pfff! My hair flew to the side of my head and the dust rose off the fridge like a blanket. I coughed. The dust slowly settled again. All I could see was coated with thick coats of it, more than I could have ever imagined. I opened my jaws and took my car in my teeth. When I had no use for it any longer the neck seemed to just disappear. That was it. I grabbed the car from my mouth and wiped the spit off of it. My prize was back! I snuck by my parents into my room where I started to bump it into the wall, except I did it lighter than before. Who says kids actually learn from their mistakes?

୧୨

I have kept my powers quite secret since I found out about it at age four. I was conscious of my powers and I had to make sure I didn't use them when my parents or anybody else who knew me was around. I had this notion in my head that if anyone found out about it, the powers could be taken away from me and given to someone else. I loved turning into animals and seeing the world the way they did, so I didn't want that to happen.

The hardest to convince that nothing was askew were my parents. They poked and prodded, keen on everything, which made it harder for me to change into my animal forms. Still, I did the impossible, kept the biggest secret that spun my life from my over-reactive parents, and lived to tell the tale.

Sometimes I even did my animal things in the room next door to my parents and they never noticed anything. That was when I thought I was invincible and nobody could figure me out. I became cocky and way too sure of myself that I wasn't careful about when or who I changed around. That's what got me into trouble the first time, and the second... and the third. Goodness! You'd think I'd learn from my mistakes!

x

Chapter 1

Deuteronomy 29:29 _(NIV)

"The secret things belong to the LORD our God, but the things revealed belong to us and to our children forever, that we may follow all the words of this law."

It was a sunny summer day when the birds were twittering and the trees were blooming and the warm breeze was blowing through the open classroom window. All the children in the classrooms were buzzing with giddy chatter on the last day of classes before summer break. We all deserved it. School was always hard for the grade one students who can't sit still for over half an hour. That was especially true today. Nobody could sit still, or stay awake. It was so hot in the classroom that everyone was sweating…well everybody except me. I had the skin of an eel on and I was cool enough. The clock ticking was driving me mad, when would the bell ring? And then, so suddenly, the school bell rang to announce the end of classes. It startled me and I joined the throng of students that poured out of the open doors of the brick school. As soon as everybody was gone, the teachers gave a sigh, the year was over and everyone had survived.

I never took the big ugly mustard yellow bus home from school, or to school for that matter, and my parents never drove me in their blue pick-up. It was assumed by everyone I knew that I walked the twenty blocks from the school back to my house. My favourite part of being part animal was that I gained their abilities when I changed. I became a fox on my way home that afternoon, partially because red foxes were common in the area, and partially because they were the fastest animal I could think of in grade one, and partially because I wanted to get home as fast as I could so I could enjoy my new-found freedom while it lasted. The only problem was that my best friend, Anne, met me as a school-book-carrying red fox as she was walking home, and almost screamed. Her eyes nearly popped out of her head and her pupils shrunk. Knowing the risk, I changed back into my own body and 'spilled the beans'. I told her everything. After that she calmed down a little and relaxed as we walked the rest of the way home together. We talked and I was glad for the long walk, so I could explain things in detail.

Anne was tall for her age and had light blonde hair that fell low on her back. Anne's parents were loving, kind people and very protective of her. Her mom was Liz, the quiet, sensitive one who loved to give and help. Her father was Paul, the loud, hardworking carpenter who doubled as a roofer and a construction worker. He loved to work with his hands while Liz loved to work with people. They were so different I was astounded that they could ever get along, but they did better than anybody else I knew.

Today Anne was dressed in the school uniform, the deep dark red plaid that could only be compared to maple leaves in the fall. It complemented her pale features. The skirt that went with it swirled in the wind and the knee-high black socks with shiny black shoes, that were considered necessary, shone in the sunlight. After I told her, and explained to her, and answered her questions, she said that she had almost already guessed because of my odd actions during class and impoliteness at lunch hour. I had even grown a tail once to help me balance while in the gymnastics unit in PE. (Nobody else had seemed to notice the three foot long lemur tail). But Anne didn't mind the new information. She took it as more secrets to our BFF friendship. But being warned not to tell anyone ever seemed to help too. The only problem is Anne was in envy of me, as you know most humans want to fly, for real. It's an amazing experience, not like falling or gliding, but really flying with the wind in your hair, dancing with it. She pleaded with me and had fell to her knees begging so what could I do? I gave her a ride on the back of a griffin, a magical creature that has the wings and head of an eagle, the legs and the tail of a lion and she loved it, after all, who else can say they've ridden on a griffin? When we got home, though, it was difficult explaining our wind blown hair and rosy cheeks.

There was only one secret I had held back from Anne and it was more than time to spill. After we got home, I called her up and asked if I could come over. She looked across the street at me out her window and gave a thumbs-up before hanging up the phone. I raced over, excited to tell her the news. When I got there, I ran to her room and closed the door.

"Anne! Guess what?" I whispered. She leaned in close.

"What?" I smiled at her.

"Do you really want to know?"

"Yes!" She screamed and I shushed her. She lowered her voice. "Tell me NOW!" She whispered fiercely.

"Okay. My name isn't really M. It's longer, and better," I paused. "...And worse." She nodded and leaned closer as my whisper grew faint.

"Morning Star," I closed my eyes and put my hands over my ears as I heard her shriek.

Anne exclaimed, "Why that's the prettiest name I've ever heard!" Her joy had been real, not forced. After all this time of hating my name I acknowledge that my view may have been wrong and that maybe it wasn't so bad after all.

"Why I thought 'M' was short for Emily or Emma or something. Morning is much, much prettier!"

"And way more uncommon," I argued, half-heartedly pouting, though I didn't really mean it. I was actually kind of proud that she liked it. My name was exotic and everyone expected me to shine or ride my golden chariot across the horizon to bring the dawn or something. I can't believe she thought I was an 'Emily'! Wow, what a common, uninteresting name, but I guess it makes sense; she thought I was 'Emm' not M.

"I love it!"

"Yeah, so did my mom. When my mom was giving birth to me, my dad was forced out of the room and the first thing he did was go get a coffee. When he came back, the first thing he said to my mom was, 'Morning, I brought the new mother her coffee. Black, cream or sugar?' But my mom heard differently. She heard 'Morning, I brought your mother coffee. Black, cream or sugar?' She thought my dad had already named me."

"Wow."

"Yah, then she said to him, 'Morning? That's a different name. Very unique. I like it.'"

"That is so cool, M. My parents got my name out of a baby book and had chosen it before I was born." Anne smiled, "You are so lucky to have a unique name. Do you know how many Anne's I've met in my life? Dozens! I don't recall ever meeting another Morning, though, especially not a Morning Star." I smiled back at her.

❧

I couldn't believe the only thing Anne asked me to do was to demonstrate to her some of her favourite animals at her house that afternoon. I argued that they would have to be common animals so her parents wouldn't get too suspicious of our secret doings. I emphasized the fact that this needed to stay secret. She only smiled.

At her house that afternoon I told her how I did so well in school. She listened politely and giggled when I had finished. I don't blame her.

"I use that silly saying, you know it? An elephant never forgets. Well, it's true. That's how I can appear not to be listening to the teachers, yet answer every question they throw at me. I use my elephant brain and I never forget a word they say. Sometimes I repeat their dumb lectures at home and it takes me forever! They are so long." I know it probably sounded stupid but that was the truth. And I really didn't want to start lying to her now.

"…And I know you get messy at lunch because animals never use utensils! They always eat with their mouths and paws, or feet. I should try it sometime."

3

She looked at me and clapped her hands at knowing so much. "I am so smart!" I laughed, imagining proper, neat Anne eating like an animal.

"Yeah but you'd look so funny with food all over your face, you are so neat and precise and never wear anything dirty or ragged." I whispered. She laughed even louder. I smiled.

I couldn't take it anymore so I giggled along with her high pitched chuckle. I laughed so long I thought I was going to burst! After a while, the laughing fit subsided and I snapped my fingers and said in a clear voice "Hyena laugh." By then Anne had stopped, too and stared not oddly but patiently.

She smiled at my excited face, "Well…"

I told her in my own voice then, to "Make me laugh. I want to show you a Hyena laugh." She looked at me strangely. "Don't worry, you'll love it!" At least I hoped she would.

"OK" She answered, "This is one of my mother's jokes. When she's all stressed out and gets frustrated with everything, she always remembers what she learned in school; Stressed spelled backwards is Desserts. She then goes out and gets me a blizzard at Dairy Queen saying over and over 'she needs desserts, she needs desserts'." My laugh that burst out then and there was a barking, braying that sounded like a monkey's snort. I stopped and I felt the Hyena in me slip away. It really had been a funny joke, sort of. I opened my hazel eyes and looked at Anne. She stared for a while but her slow smile gradually spread across her pale pink lips and brightened the room. Her blue eyes blinked as she sat in amazed silence. I paced over to the chair and sat down, waiting for her feedback on what I had just done. I though maybe I had done something wrong as the silence stretched on and just when I was going to move to get up, she spoke in a soft but excited squeak.

"That was amazing!" Her voice said it all. She loved it! I knew then that I could always get a smile out on her face if I used my impressions and that little Hyena laugh. I heard footsteps outside the door and I snapped my head to the left. Just then her mother walked in. Liz was tall with short almond brown hair. Her glasses were thin and made her look smart. Her voice was soft and kind.

"Hi Mrs. Walters," I twiddled my thumbs, which was a dead give-away, "What's up?" I knew my comment wasn't the best considering my animal noises. I had already been told they were 'very loud and obnoxious'.

"Hello M." Liz said softly, looking around in bewilderment. "Is everyone alright? I heard some strange noises coming from here." She cocked her head, and looked at each of us, determined to get the truth. She pointed her finger and I smiled crookedly at her.

"Oh, mother wasn't she awesome? Morning can make any animal sound you can think of! She is truly amazing! Would you do an imitation for mother, Morning?" I took a long breath. Anne told her mom the truth in a way that didn't make me seem like a freak. I had to owe it to her, she had just preformed a miracle.

"Sure Anne, I'd love to." I replied, taking a deep breath. I had to make something sound realistic, without scaring Anne's mother. "What animal would you like me to imitate, Mrs. Walters?" I turned my head to look her in the eye. A smile instantly lit up her face. Her cheeks turned a rosy pink.

"Why, it wouldn't inconvenience you would it, M?" I shook my head and my curls flew into my face. I brushed them away hastily. "Well, I've always wanted to hear an elephant." She quirked her head, thinking for a bit. "But I don't need noise. No, never mind M. Save the sounds for the game you and Anne are playing. Have fun, you two, and don't make the noise too loud again. Your father is working and shouldn't be disturbed. Make them a little quieter, can you do that, M?"

"Yes, Mrs. Walters. I'll try to keep the noise down." I gave her a salute.

She smiled, waved and walked out of the room. From then on, she avoided us when I was making my noises. Maybe she was afraid of them or was afraid they were hurting Anne, but she kept her distance. Anyway this gave me the leeway to turn into exotic types of animal's right in Anne's very own bedroom. Although, for some of the bigger ones, we had to push the bed back against the wall.

Everyday after that I would imitate any animal Anne desired and she would giggle her heart out. It was the life. I loved Anne's laugh. It always made me smile. Over the summer vacation we spent every hour of every day together. When school started again in the fall we walked to and from school together. We did schoolwork together and I helped her with her work and memorizing techniques. After we finished our homework, we'd go hide away in her room and I'd impress her with new animals each day. Sometimes I even read up on interesting facts that went along with the animal. Some were silly like, 'Did you know that cats in Nova Scotia have a high probability of having six toes?' She'd laugh and the world would be great. Sometimes, but not very often, Anne would search up a quirky fact for me, too. I'll never forget this one. 'Did you know reindeer like to eat bananas?' It was the funniest one I have ever heard. And it was so random. She just came up to me in the middle of class and told me. I was giggling for the rest of the day. (Yes, I did get in trouble with the teachers, but the 'would-you-like-to-share-this-with-the-class-if-you-think-it's-so-funny' thing worked for me. I told the class and they loved it. I even saw the teacher hide a grin... But I still got punished.)

Anne and I were inseparable. We were the kids at school people pushed in line to sit with. We helped people and weren't bullies. We frequently stood up to a bully or two and were the unbeatable duo at king's court. We were always king and queen, and we took turns being either one. We always beat everyone out of our court, and we thought we always would. That was, until I had to be transferred to a different school during grade five. I was heartbroken when I heard and I can swear I cried that entire summer. I told Anne as she was walking to school the first day of grade six after summer. I told her and then I was shipped off to a public school across town that was cheaper than the private Christian school we went to together.

She made new friends; I did too… sort of… not really, but I never told her that. I never forgot Anne's laugh and we were just as close (maybe even closer) friends and we were still just across the street. We called each other every day and talked for hours about the ongoing events in our different schools. Sometimes, I'd even recite a lecture or two or rattle off a chapter I'd read in a book so that she'd relax. When I moved schools it nearly tore her apart. Although we didn't see each other every day we thought about each other and talked to each other. And, as it's said, 'absence makes the heart grow fonder'. We were extremely close. We had a sleepover almost every weekend, and visited randomly to catch up on events and news. That is when our mom's became friends. Good friends. They couldn't bear to see us apart, so they had get-togethers just so we could get together. It was so nice of them to do that for us. They had more to talk about then than we did and all the time spent together helped our bond grow stronger, although I was Anne-sick all day in class and during the lonely recess and lunch times. I missed her so much. We even made friendship bracelets to remember each other by when we weren't together.

Chapter II

Psalm 119:105 (NIV)
"Your word is a lamp to my feet and a light for my path."

A year later, we both joined an Awana group. We attended regularly and missed each other dearly when one of us couldn't be there. (Awana is a Christian organization where young kids get together to learn about God. Awana stands for Approved Workmen Are Not Ashamed.) Usually we started with a prayer and then moved onto games. My favourite game was 'Bowla'. Bowla was a game of stamina. And it would help if you hadn't eaten a big meal before, too. The needed materials were a rope, a sock and two tennis balls. The rope was tied to the sock and in the sock were the tennis balls. The 'it' would lie on the ground and swing the contraption around his/her head. The rest of the group huddled around and jumped over the rope when it came their way. The 'it' could stop it suddenly and switch directions and speed up or slow down. Whoever fell, then or got their shoe or foot caught in the rope was out. The last person standing got a prize and became the next 'it'. I always asked the Commander if we were playing 'Bowla' every meeting. We also did a lot of relays and races. Another game I was good at was the chicken game. Everyone likes the chicken game. It was also cool when Anne and I got to be on the same team. It was uncool when we had to fight against each other but we were so evenly matched that it usually ended in a tie.

After games we'd go downstairs for another short prayer and Bible memorizing time. We each got a workbook and we had to go through it, page by page. That was the hard part for me. Because at my last school, where we had both gone to, we had to memorize Bible verses, (so Anne already knew some). At my new school, we didn't even see a bible throughout the whole year. Silly public schools. My favourite bible verse was Psalm 119:105. My father used to sing it to me when I was little and I liked it because it spoke of lights in the darkness and paths of your life. I couldn't wait to choose my path then, although I knew it would have something to do with my animal powers.

Anne and I went to Awana to be together, but to also meet new friends. We met many girls and a few boys and had competitions where we saw who could memorize the most verses in one night. I usually lost, but it was fun for me to beat my own record. The evenings usually ended around 8pm. By the end of the night, I was plum tuckered out. I never cheated in Awana. I never became animals to help me win; it was fun playing fair and square and even more fun when I won fair. Anne noticed and was proud of me, she said it was brave and showed that I had courage not to use my powers when it would be so easy to. I blushed when she said that and replied with a hasty thanks.

∽

My new school was one community away from my house, and a forever walk away from home. It was a ten minute drive. It would have been about an hour walk. For the first time in my short life, my parents needed something to hold me after school, or so they thought. They decided on an out-of-school-care system three blocks away from the new school. It was close enough so that I could walk there after school. It was cheap, and it was experienced. My parents thought it was perfect. I didn't. I never even got past the front hallway. The place gave me the creeps, and no wonder, it had animal pelts and heads and butts on every wall. Mom knew of my love for animals and took me aside in the hall, ten steps from the door. The animal's eyes pierced my back with daggers of sadness and hate, as I turned to my mother. I looked out the door and kept my eye on a butterfly as she knelt down in front of me. I thought if these people knew about me I could be the next victim to hang in shame on that wall.

"Would you stay here if I registered you?" I turned to look at her. Her eyes told me that she wouldn't care if the answer was 'no'. So I told her the truth while starting to cry.

"Mom," I kept looking from the window to her eyes. "Mom I hate it here, it gives me the creeps. If you were a girl who loved animals, would you want to stay in this slaughter house every day after school when you could be at home having fun and being happy?" The tears freely flowed and I tried to bolt for the door. Mom caught my hand.

"You won't have to stay here, sweetie, but to be polite, we will walk out as politely as we walked in." I shimmied out the door and mom let go of my hand as I ran for the car.

From then on, I was allowed to stay home alone. I was a responsible girl who never got into trouble, although, just in case, I still wasn't allowed to use the stove until grade ten.

∽

At first I thought life without Anne would be dreadful and I spent many a night on my wet pillow taking in deep breaths and hiccupping from all the crying. I learned life goes on. Seven years after I changed schools, we were both seniors in high school and graduation was in two more days. I was at home one night. This is the night I had my first adventure without Anne, even though the outcome of this journey could affect us all.

It was dark and stormy when I was supposed to be in bed. I couldn't doze off no matter how hard I tried. The lightning would brighten up my whole room, showing strange shadows on the walls from objects on my dresser. The thunder would shake the entire house. I huddled under the covers, content in keeping my eyes closed and my ears plugged. What a white night!

At first I didn't hear it. It was soft and gradually became a boom. It was a knock at the door. I pretended to snore which was totally obvious I was faking because I don't snore. Never have, never will.

A slow fading voice whispered, "M...t ...e ...tsi... in ...ee ...in...s." Thunder boomed around me and I thought I began to think I had imagined it. The more I thought about it, the more one idea came to mind.

I gasped, sitting up with the covers rumpled around me, "Wha-at?" I was annoyed with the voice; it was probably Seth, my older brother playing a prank on me. But the more I thought about it, the more uneasy I got. He wouldn't do something like that, *would* he?

The voice waited to respond, and I became a nervous wreck. I wiped sweat off my forehead with my sleeve and flung back the covers only to get a cold blast of air. I pulled the covers back on as the voice spoke. I became deathly quiet this time, and held still, trying to figure out if it was Seth. I could just imagine those blue eyes laughing at the thought that I was scared of him. "Meet me outside in three minutes." The voice definitely wasn't Seth's. I slowly stood up.

"And what happens if I don't?" I replied in a squeaky voice because of my fear.

"Then the barker is let out, you're punishment." Coco! She ran away if you weren't watching her when she went out to pee. The stranger was going to let her loose! All of a sudden my fear was replaced with anger and worry about my dog.

"Coming," I answered slowly. I got up and put my clothes on my eyes fixed on the door. It stayed shut. I latched my belt and I brushed my hair. A shaky hand slowly reached for the door knob. It swung open in my face. I had quick reflexes. I transformed into a dog and slid behind the door, my breathing quick and shallow. I thought of Ephesians chapter 6 from Awana. I prayed to put on the armour of God. I prayed for Him to help me. With God on our side, we can make it (Psalm 24). A head stuck around the corner. It was a boy, my older brother Seth. I was myself again in an instant and flung him on the bed, he almost screamed.

"Morning! Don't scare me like that! Did you see the wacky little kid who was wandering around in here? He was asking me what room you were in. I was half asleep and told him, but seconds later I woke and wondered what he wanted.

"Ya, I'm going out to meet him," I glanced down at my glow-in-the-dark watch, "Two minutes ago." I busied myself with tying my boots.

"What's wrong? Did he threaten you? Why are you going out on a stormy night to meet a stranger?" My brother's concern was touching, considering the fact that he ignores me most of the time. He is in University and thinks he's so much better than high-school-ers.

"Ya, he said he was going to let Coco out. He had said something along the lines of punishment or something. But don't worry, it's him who's getting the punishment tonight." I replied walking out of my room and down the hall, Seth at my heels. "Once I call his parents or the police he'll think twice about breaking and entering a strangers house on a dare or for a prank or whatever, but he'll regret it." I reached the living room. It was trashed. "Looks like we've got some cleaning up to do before we go back to bed tonight." Seth gave a weak smile and asked where Coco was and if she was still in the house. I peeked into her pen and it looked like she was asleep. "Hold on one moment I've got to talk to her." I jumped into her pen and dog-morphed for the second time tonight. I woke her and asked if she'd seen a man in here. She replied that a small asparagus had run through here. He had been chased by a tomato. Then squashes bopped behind them singing a silly song. I told her she'd been dreaming. She fell asleep in my paws. I shook my head; no more Veggie Tales before bed ever again. I pulled my paws out from under her and sparrow-morphed. "Seth, which is easier to see in the dark, a sparrow or a dove." I asked him when I already knew the answer. I un-morphed even before he answered my question. We were outside by now and I was shivering in the cold. I should have brought a coat. I dove-morphed just as his voice came back.

"Huh? Oh, dove," he had replied with an absent mind. I couldn't help but wonder where exactly his mind was absent to. Boys these days! Probably some stupid boy thing, like 'my feet are cold, I should have put on boots.'

"I don't see our strange intruder," I told Seth. "Maybe he ran off. He didn't even touch my dog." We walked out onto the back deck. The motion-sensing lights in our backyard came on, leaving ghostly shadows of lawn chairs in the blue light. The open barbeque lid looked like a menacing monster, ready to chomp. I went over and closed it, I can't believe mom forgot to again. I shivered and bird-perched on the railing.

"That is very strange. Maybe it was a trick." Seth offered. I thought for a second flew to the door. I became human again and reached for the handle, only to find the door was locked.

"I'm glad you came, I got tired waiting." The voice startled me and I spun around with my fists in the air ready for a fight. A figure stepped out of the trees and leaves rustled in the breeze that just came up. It all added to the sinister atmosphere. I felt Seth beside me pull his fists up, too. His extra inches in height were comforting. "You harm me, I harm little miss pooch-paws." His tone was cold, as he pointed to a matted mess that emerged at his side, so were his deep-blue eyes. They were almost ice as he glared at me. His hair fell knotted around his dark face. His greasy hand was on my dog's thick green leash with a limp coco attached. She looked like she'd been beaten to a pulp. I became a dog and called to the limp puppy with warning barks, telling her that she was in danger. She flashed her teeth and her red eyes glowed in the dark with tiny fires igniting in her pupils. She glowered at me and I saw that this wasn't my dog. I trotted over to the man, changing into a human millimetres from his nose. Now I was standing face to face with the intruder. I saw his eyes widen at the sight of my sudden change in size. I was a whole inch and a half taller than him, but I realized it wasn't a young boy; it was an older man, older than Seth. He took a step backwards. In a high-pitched, fearful squeak, he said, "It's true, you're not just a legend. The beast is in the human world!" I waited for his antics to end before posing my questions.

"You are...who? You know me...how? I'm *what* since...when? You are here...why? And..." I pointed to the lump of evil. "That is...what? It's certainly not my dog!" With each pause I'd stepped closer to the man and he'd stepped back. I had pointed my finger between his eyes and maybe spat a little on him in my rage. I felt Seth step protectively closer every time I stepped away. Even though he was older and was taller by three inches and bugged me like nobody ever could, it felt good that he would protect me. Or so he thought he would.

The stranger just smiled and replied using magic. "You're coming with me." I shouted at Seth to duck and stay out of the way. A billow of smoke flared through the night. I became an eagle and flew out of the way just as a large net flew through the air, hidden by the immense cloud. I turned and faced him, talons out and flew towards his head. He readied himself for the eagle with a long spear but instead was sat on by an elephant, the spear clattering to the ground and rolling until it fell of the side of the deck. It gave a quiet thump as it hit the grass. I smiled to myself, my transformations were getting quicker. Lumbering off the poor boy, I twisted into bat. Bat was a good night warrior. I could use my echo-location to find my target and my black suit blended in with my surrounding darkness. I found Seth and told him it was okay. Trembling and with no idea how I'd handled the mess, Seth stood up. He coughed and blinked from the retreating smoke, waving his hand in front of his face.

"Who was he?" Seth asked, half crazed, "Has this happened before to you?"

I shook my head, back in my own body. "No, I don't know who he is." I looked closer at the unconscious man. "I have never, ever seen him before. I don't think he's from around here." I felt goose-bumps start to form on my arms and legs, suddenly aware of the breeze. "Help me lift him. I think we should take him out to the end of the driveway, at least."

"Maybe even further. I don't want to be anywhere near him." Seth stared at the man and took a cautious step. I grabbed him by the wrists and lifted, motioning for Seth to take his feet. Seth, being much taller, lifted the ankles way too high, so the boy was awkwardly tipped.

"P.U! His socks stink!" Seth voiced, raising the boy's feet even higher. I buckled under the extra weight and leaned down to get a better grip on his wrists. Now he was almost vertical.

Plink! A small, silver object fell out of the breast pocket in his plaid long-sleeved shirt. I picked it up and put it in my back pocket. Seth and I scuffed down our driveway with the boy strung between us. We lightly laid him down on the grassy island on the other side of our street. Coincidentally, the same grassy space Anne and I had picnicked at the day before. It was two doors down from her house. I hoped she was getting her sleep tonight. Lightning flashed and the boy mumbled a bit. Seth froze. I didn't dare to breathe. We slowly stepped away and I slipped on the dewy grass and fell on my behind. The boy's metal thing dug into my hip. I took it out of my pocket to look at it closer. The boy finished stirring and went back to sleep. That must have been some fall. Seth helped me up as I rolled the thing in my hand. It was a relatively heavy object the size of a pen. There was a single, small switch at the bottom, like a pop-out pen would have. I was hesitant to push the button. What if it wasn't a pen. What if it was a knife or something dangerous? Curiosity took over my fear and before I had time to think again, I pushed it and held the stick arms length away. It slowly started to glow and lengthen, like a TV antenna. It glowed a reddish orange and vibrated in my hand, making a soft buzzing sound. I felt a jolt as it gave my sleepy body energy I didn't know I had. Seth looked over, but didn't really seem to see. He had his eyes trained on the boy and if he even twitched, Seth jumped.

I held the thing in one hand and touched it to the grass. It buzzed again and that spot looked greener than all around it. I pushed the button on the bottom once again and the thing stopped glowing and retracted back to it's pen size. I was amazed. I had never seen anything like it before. I wondered where the stranger got it from. I slowly knelt down and put it back into the boy's pocket. I paused thinking that that kind of power in the wrong hands could be terrifying. I rushed as my pinkie brushed against his shirt and stood up in a hurry, bumping into Seth behind me. I fell on top of him and looked at the stars in the sky. The storm was clearing. The stars were shining bright, and I could see the big dipper and Orion's belt.

"You okay?" Seth's head was a black circle that blotted out the twinkling lights above. I nodded and jumped to my feet.

"I'm fine, just a little spooked. That's all." I brushed myself off and started towards the house. I crossed the street and the pavement shook with the force of my footsteps.

Seth followed me, him in bare feet crossing the same cold hard rock I was in comfy boots. "You do know we're still locked out, right?" I nodded, chewing on one of my nails. I grew it into a bear claw and bit it so it looked like the house key. I reached for the deadbolt and stuck my nail in the key slot. I twisted my nail, pain searing through my finger as my nail felt like it was being ripped off. But the pain was worth it. It worked. The lock turned and Seth hurried inside ahead of me and made a beeline for his room and his soft, warm bed. I walked in after him and closed the door, making sure it was locked from the inside. The next project was cleaning up the torn apart living room. With the energy lent from the glowing stick I finished cleaning in record time. Two hours later the room was spotless, the energy rush was gone. The adrenaline had faded. I fell onto the couch and closed my eyes, promising myself that I would wake up again in ten minutes and go to bed. I dreamed peacefully until the sunlight woke me up the next morning.

Chapter III

Psalm 62:3 (NIV)

"How long will you assault a man? Would all of you throw him down–
this leaning wall, this tottering fence?"

Almost immediately after I woke I sensed that something was wrong. Call it animal instinct or whatever you want but I was on edge from eye-open. After sneaking around the house, I figured out why. My parent's bed was empty and made. Racing through the hallway, I found that Seth was missing, too. A quick check of his drawers confirmed the fact that they had gone. Gone and packed their stuff. I hoped Seth hadn't told them about my animal transformations. I grabbed my emergency backpack from my room and skidded past the kitchen. I became a mouse in a hurry and peeked into the room. A man, **the** man, was fiddling with a many-wired device that he stuck to the fridge. He bent down as I snuck up behind him. I became human to see the note on the table that my mother had left for me about the family's quick departure.

> Hi Honey,
> We are going to the cottage.
> We decided to let you sleep. Get your rest, hon.
> Seth said you had a late night last night.
> I understand if you sleep in.
> We will expect you by suppertime.
> Take your time and come when you are ready.
> Love you,
> MOM

I looked towards the fridge as something clattered to the ground. The boy was busy on the contraption. I backed up slowly, and then turned quickly to leave when I bumped into a chair. He had turned around in an instant, but I was already gone. I raced to the back door and flung it open. It banged against the wall and left a small dent. I remember thinking, 'I'm in so much trouble if mom and dad find out. I have to fix that.' I ran outside into the warm

15

morning air. Placing my hands on the deck railing, I heaved myself over using my running momentum. Landing at a run after the three foot drop I heard the back door slam again. I pictured the angry man jumping the fence after me and being surprised at the drop. I didn't bother looking back as I heard him squeal. He had twisted his ankle. But when he landed, I was already at the playhouse in our backyard. I went in, closing the door neatly behind me, and jumped out the always open side window, slamming the pane down and ripping my shirt. The edge of it had gotten caught in the window. I became a tiny little bird and flew quickly into the bush beside the playhouse to think about it as the boy got up. I peeked out of the lush leafiness and saw him making a head first ram into the door.

"It's a pull door, not a push." I whispered, giggling at him. He rubbed his head and pulled at the door, but with all that anger he pulled too hard and the little door came off it's hinges. Throwing it away he stomped into the playhouse, being extra careful of the low ceiling. I heard a 'thud' and looked to see the door landed under the deck. Ironically it landed on the firewood pile; which was exactly where it would have ended up, anyway, now that it was wrecked. The boy saw the window and the torn piece of my clothing and I shrunk into the heart of the bush. I felt the vibration from my perch as he forced the window open and grabbed at the piece of my shirt. I shouldn't have left it there. That's how people find who they're looking for when they are tracking them. I knew that this was worse than the movies, because the tracker was the bad guy and I was the tracked. He shook the shred in anguish and then he noticed me. Me, the cute, innocent little bird who minds her own business and who doesn't really want to fight a big scary human. I cowered in the bush until the boy came out and I figured if I acted more like a bird, it would be more believable that I was one. Singing, I fluttered to the branch three inches from his nose. The boy held still. I cocked my head and chirped at him. I think I had finally convinced him I was a real bird when I had to go and ruin it.

He was turning away as I spoke. "Are you ever going to get it!" He turned around and I leaped as a jaguar out of the bush, knocking him to the ground. I batted playfully at his face and left some claw marks before racing away.

I padded around the garage on silent paws and stopped at the fence that bordered the alley. "Ugh!" The boy must have tripped over my brother's golf club, because it soon came flying past the edge of the garage, nowhere near where I was. Thankfully. It landed on the concrete walk in the backyard that led to the deck. *Clang!*

I thought about it, and I would almost say that this was fun, seeing the boy so mad about something. That was hardly fair. I felt so bad but the bad feeling went away as he stomped around the corner and huffed at me, crossing his arms. He looked so funny like that, I could barely stop myself from laughing. A grown man, huffing and having a temper tantrum like a boy!

He looked older than he had last night. My best guess is that he would be a decade older than me. I was in grade twelve, sixteen this summer. So he must be in university or college, if he was smart enough to be let in. Maybe he wanted to get back at Seth for a prank he'd played at SAIT, but last night my brother had denied knowing him. That only meant one thing. **He was here for me.**

"WHAT DO YOU WANT?" I asked in the loudest panther voice I could manage. No matter how much enunciation I gave my words, as cats, they always come out roar-ish.

"I want your pelt. It is legend that your pelt, that is your **skin**..." He waited to see my response. A normal girl might have screamed, but I rolled my eyes. "Anyway, your pelt, if hanged on the wall in the castle of Dovera, will be the sight of the century. It is said, that every full moon your pelt, if hung in the castle, my castle, will change to be the pelt of a different animal. You have been a legend for longer than my father has had his beard. I will prove to him I am man enough to take over the kingdom as the new ruler when I bring him your pelt." I stood up as a human again and took a step backwards towards the fence.

"How did you find me?"

"Oh, that has taken my whole life. First I had to prove you were real, then I had to find what world you were in and when I found this big world, I had to find where you were in it. It was a long, difficult task, but it will be worth it when you are hanging over the fireplace in my throne room. It will be my life's dream come true."

I took another step back as he drew an arrow. "Well keep dreaming." I changed my legs into kangaroo legs and jumped the fence in an instant. I flew over the fence and then became a tiny mouse and huddled my back against it. I felt vibrations from the arrow hitting the wood and looked around to see the arrow in the fence where I was standing not a second before. I dared to breathe as I heard scrambling as the man was trying to heave himself over the fence. He needed some upper-body muscle, so if you ask me, he needed to play outside more, or go to a gym and work-out. I heard him curse as his pant leg got caught on a protruding nail and ripped. He fell onto the ground, inches from my whiskers, and noticed me at once. 'Not a game, not a game.' I kept repeating to myself. This wasn't fun anymore, now that I knew he wanted me dead to put in a castle so he could become king. I twitched my whiskers and gave a little squeak.

"Ha," The boy taunted. "Now I'm bigger than you, mouse. If you really were a mouse, you'd be scared to death." His breath stank!

"Well I'm not really a mouse. And I'm not afraid of you." His hand reached out to grab me, but I bit it. I raced through a slit in the fence and used my squirrel form to climb the tree. I used my claws to force my little body up the tree beside the fence. I climbed up as arrows whizzed past me. At one point, there was another squirrel that scurried beside me and then out onto the electrical wire. I flew as a magpie to the other side of the alley and scared a real magpie back across the alley that landed on the garage roof. I saw a flash and heard a bang at the same time and then a helpless squawk. I looked, but now I wish I hadn't. The boy had shot the magpie. He had taken a pistol out of his shirt and shot the poor magpie as it sat innocently on the roof. It could have been me, but he killed an innocent creature. It rolled off the roof and he walked over and knelt beside it. Now I was really mad.

I jumped out of the tree and landed on strong goat legs that disappeared as soon as the dust settled. The dust disappeared, revealing my tattered blue sneakers with a frayed toe. My face was on fire, my anger spreading to the rest of my body.

Now this is really odd. When I'm really mad, I mean *really,* really mad, not just angry. When I'm mad, I blink, not like a light bulb, not like eyelids. I don't blink like a lumbering train or a speeding hummer. The way I blink is wacky, and unique, but only I can do it. When I am really angry, the anger is released in the fiercest animals I can be. For less than half a second I am this animal, then I am another, and I keep changing until my anger is gone. It's quite a sight. I once did it to my brother and he was scared of me for weeks.

Still, this boy did something ten times worse than what Seth did. He was enjoying trying to catch me, and I was enjoying getting away, but this was serious. He killed an innocent creature that God had lovingly made and he ransacked the living room after breaking into my house. I was infuriated. Blinking with all my power and force, I hoped it would do something bad to him. But the thing about revenge is that, no matter how much poison you drink, it isn't going to kill the other person; it will only make you miserable. Revenge will sicken your stomach and life will lose it's purpose. No matter how angry I got or how hard I blinked, it would never affect the boy.

He pointed the pistol at me, but still I stood. I waited for the shot as I blinked through one set of animals after another. I opened my eyes. The gun was hanging at his side.

He was cowering but looking me straight in the eyes, the blue-ish gray-ness pierced through my heart and soul, and I felt almost sorry for him. Out on an endless hunt to impress his father so he could run the kingdom. I looked closer and saw in his eyes his emotions. He only seemed taken aback. I was surprised when my anger was all let out that he wasn't that afraid. He was a pretty good actor, though, he almost had me fooled. I really thought

I'd scared him…until I saw the smile. It started in his eyes, a small twinkle, then spread across his lips. He stood up straight from his cowering position and stared at me in amazement.

He took a step toward me and I grew fangs. "You're more powerful than I thought." His quiet voice had changed from hunger for my pelt to…kindness? "I have to tell dad." Then he ran. Past me, across the alley, tripping on the loose stones. He opened the garbage box of a nearby house and jumped inside. It thumped down behind him and I suddenly noticed how quiet it was. The gunshot had probably scared off the other birds, it had probably scared the neighbours, too. I made a split-second decision to follow him. Curiosity was taking over me; I couldn't control my legs, even though I was strangely in my own. My sneakers raced across the pebbles and my legs pumped with the effort to keep up.

I soon found myself in front of the garbage box with my fingers gliding over the peeling surface of the painted wood. I lifted it slowly, but I felt that it wasn't an ordinary garbage box. It seemed different (no smell of rotting food). I put the other strap of my backpack on my shoulder, took a deep breath, said a silent prayer that I wasn't falling into his trap, and stepped inside.

Chapter IV

Isaiah 40:31 _(KJV)
"But they that wait upon the LORD shall renew their strength;
They shall mount up with wings as eagles; They shall run,
and not be weary; and they shall walk, and not faint."

The first thing I felt was a cool breeze. It blew my hair around and howled fiercely through the boulders around me. I opened my eyes and saw a dull, cloudy day. The breeze was a lot colder than the warm, humid, suffocating one I had just left. I untied my sweater from around my waist. I was prepared. I put it on and decided to figure out where I was. I certainly wasn't still in the alley, or the garbage box. I was very far away. But where was I?

The dirt around me was a reddish orange. It was fine and soft. It wasn't fertile, it was more like sand. I stood up and brushed the red dust off my backside. It was sandstone, neatly ground sandstone. The garden rocks back home were sandstone, that's the only reason I recognized it.

When I was standing, the first thing I saw was the clouds. They were fluffy cumulus, but were dark like nimbus. I'm no meteorologist, but I say wherever I was, I was in for a summer squall, or a big thunderstorm. The dark clouds meant rain, and the fluffy meant it had been a warm week of evaporation to cause it. I started to panic, I had to find shelter, although it was barren on this rock I was on. I started to walk, keeping my eye on the clouds and almost missed the cliff.

The hard, rocky ground I was on made it hard to walk. I'd twist my ankle and stub my toe, but when I put my foot down and there was nothing there, I fell on my butt. I fell on my butt with my feet dangling over the edge. Freezing, I felt my legs sway over the edge helplessly. I rolled onto my stomach and slowly got up, my knees on solid ground. Standing slowly, I stepped back. I looked at the land around me. It was lush. Many trees and forests dotted the landscape. One was right below. Below me maybe 200 feet! I was on a piece of rock that jutted out from the rest of the cliff. It looked like it could have been a broken off bridge over the valley, but it was too cloudy to see to the other side. The winds started to blow fiercely. I had to find shelter, or I could be blown right off the edge in the storm.

I looked down, where was shelter? The trees might block out the wind, but they wouldn't keep out the whipping rain. They were forests of lush deciduous trees, in full bloom. The green leaves were full of chlorophyll and the fruits produced, far below, were fully ripe and big and I could see the tastiness with my eagle eyes. I looked and saw the patchwork yellows and browns of fields with crops I couldn't name, but so full that they were in no comparison to the ones back home.

I stood there looking for two full minutes, the wind battering against me was fierce, but it seemed calm as I looked out over the new land. Soon, as suddenly as the winds had started, they stopped. I remembered an old saying that it was always calm before the storm. Then a light drizzle started and the winds picked up again, howling fiercely. I jumped off the cliff and was caught by strong, firm wings; the wings of an eagle, *my* wings. I thought about the verse in the bible that says 'those who wait upon the Lord will rise up on wings as eagles'. I don't think they meant me, but who knows? God does, but it's not like He'll tell me anything about the future. That would ruin the surprise of life.

I looked back at the cliff and noticed a small cave dug into the rock…I wonder where that goes, I thought. Out of the corner of my eye I saw something move. I looked and saw the man scrabbling down the side of the cliff on a little path worn into the stone by goats that were in front of him. He was struggling to stay on the small path as the winds blew him first one way, then another. The goats seemed to be fine, but I wondered who the man was. It kept bugging me, but I had to find shelter first, then find the mysterious man. The rain pelted my face… well, the eagle's face, but it still hurt. I slowly tipped so that the winds would blow me down into the valley with the forest. At first it seemed far away, but as I fell, it came closer and closer, jumping up to catch me. I misjudged the distance to the nearest tree and tumbled, head first, into its strong branches. I turned back into me and sat there until my racing heartbeat slowed.

ℰℐ

I found shelter in the crook of a tree and fell asleep as soon as my head hit the bark. I was in deep slumber when the tree branches swayed and curled around me and cradled me. Then the tree twisted so its bark blocked out the wind and rain from my face. I slept there all night, cradled by a moving tree and before I knew it, I was dreaming.

I dreamed the entire night of the man coming to get me. First, we were at home and I was picking up the strange pen, then were battling in a fiery fortress and we were fighting over the glowing pen. I dreamed he was shaking his fists at me as I flew on wings as eagles away from him and the cliff and all the problems I ever had. I dreamed I was flying toward the lush landscape I saw before, and Anne, and back towards my family, but I felt something behind me, and then it shot a bullet at me. I was the magpie the man had killed and I was wounded and falling... falling... falling toward the rocks below. I got a fluttery feeling in my stomach and then felt the force of the impact. I felt the impact of the ground, but I couldn't get up, I couldn't move, I couldn't even open my eyelids from the horrible dream. All I could do was lie there and take in the horrifying scene before my eyes, projecting on the back of my eyelids. I saw the dead bird, and then it became me, and then it was the boy, and then it was the new land I was in. A montage of images flew through my mind, so fast that I couldn't recognize some of them. I squirmed and tried to get out of it. I finally gave up and peace washed over me... and then I woke up.

When I had started to squirm, the tree was surprised. When I rolled over and fell, screaming in my dreams, it felt horrible that it had let me drop. It gently picked me up and held me in its branches, trying to sooth me, trying to calm my thoughts. I cried in my sleep and called out for help, but still the tree held me close, curving the twigs around me so I wouldn't fall again. Soon other trees were awake and marvelling over the screaming human clasped in the crooked branches of their friend. They slid their roots over so they could be closer to it, wondering what it was doing. Feeling helpless, they sang a soothing song to the rustling rhythm of their branches and leaves in the wind, some even danced. After a while I stopped making noise and they all sighed their approval. The tree then cradled me closer, like a mother cradling her child and the others leaned in closer to watch over me.

My eyelids opened and I saw beautiful sunlight flitting through the trees. I saw branch after branch over my head. *Funny,* I thought, *I don't remember that many branches above me last night.* I was lying on my back, face up, on soft leaves sprouting out of wrinkled branches. I was in a sort of hammock, held, swaying, between two branches of an even bigger tree. All around me, trees were *leaning close?* I looked at one of them and, in a trick of the light, the marks on the bark sort of looked like a face. Then, it did the weirdest thing. It **smiled** at me. I got up and backed away.

"Hello young human." It said to me, "How was your sleep? I've been told my branches are the most comfortable." I opened my mouth and left it hanging as I watched the tree speak. I backed up some more and bumped into another tree. I jumped and turned.

"What," it asked me, "Never seen a talking tree before?"

"No," I answered, "Where I come from trees don't talk." It slid closer to me, its roots pulling it forward through the ground. "O-o-or move." I took a step back to the tree with the hammock.

"It must be a pretty still, boring place, then." It said, sliding closer. A branch from the hammock tree wrapped around my waist and pulled me away from the other tree.

"Quit scaring her. If trees don't talk where she's from, so what? Leave her alone!" It un-twisted its branches and the hammock disappeared. It looked at me. "You are very young. What are you doing in the woods alone?"

"I'm lost."

"I can see that." The tree replied. "Otherwise you wouldn't have been here. Most of your kind are afraid of the woods, they are afraid of trees."

"I'm not," I replied. "I kind of like the woods. It feels nice having such big, strong trees around me, even back home; looking at trees in a park was one of my favourite things to do. And I'm not as young as you think. I'm eighteen years old."

"How old do you think *I* am?" asked the tree. I had no idea. "I'm almost three hundred years old. Compared to me, you're young." I nodded.

"You must have seen a lot. Do you know how to get back to Earth?"

The tree looked at me closer. "If you go that way..." The tree pointed with one of its branches, "If you walk and walk, you'll eventually get somewhere."

"Yeah," piped up the tree behind me, "If you go anywhere you're bound to get somewhere, right? You can never be nowhere."

I nodded. "That makes sense. Thank you." The trees smiled again. I patted their bark. "Thanks." I walked in the direction the tree had pointed.

"Nice girl." I heard one say as I passed.

"Very nice girl," the other agreed. The trees from then on slid away to give me a clear path. I took my time at first, looking at all the unique plants. They all looked surprised to see me and would talk about me and gossip behind my back.

"Look, a girl. We haven't had a girl in the forest since..." and "Oh, isn't she pretty, she reminds me of..." and "What's she doing here, humans never come this far into the woods..." Some would slither up to look at me, some would slide away and ignore me, but all the trees and plants moved, and all of them talked. Every face was different and I marvelled at how the bark made it so that you could see the outlines of what looked like a human face. Some of the bushes bounded up to me and acted like dogs. Some would rustle and stick their leaves up and bound away.

Then I started to run through the fresh greenery as dew dropped on my head and insects buzzed by my ear and sun danced beside me through the trees; some of the trees danced beside me, too. Stopping in a clearing, I looked up at the clear blue sky with thin wispy clouds. A whole new world was at my fingertips. I could explore, I could meet new people, I could… hold on. I would have to avoid people, lest anyone tell the man or his father, the king, about me. Then I could be in danger. I sat down on the soft grass to think it over. With my head in my hands, I felt my back tingle. Someone was watching me. I slowly turned my head and used my super-sensitive bat ears to listen.

I heard the footsteps of a human with fairly large feet. It sounded like a man, but it could be a lady without high heels.

"Who's there?" The sounds stopped as the human froze. I stood with my knees bent, ready to fly away if it was the evil boy again. I did a whole 360 and paused, but I wasn't facing my shadow, which I soon found out was a big mistake. I couldn't tell if anybody were to come up behind me, and someone did.

I stood there, silent and waiting for nearly two minutes. Suddenly, I felt a squeezing around my waist and I was lifted off the ground. I squirmed and kicked and screamed. I had flown before, but never as a human.

"Oh quit screaming Nora, it's only me, Dawn." I continued screaming. I had no idea who Nora was and I was positive that I wasn't her.

When the strange man, Dawn, got around to setting me down on firm soil, I spun around as he exclaimed, "I win…" He stopped, however, when he saw me. Dawn stepped closer for a better look. I also took another look. He was relatively tall and really handsome and maybe a year or two older than me. Our eyes met and he looked away. "You're not Nora."

"No, I don't believe I am. I'm M." I stuck out my hand and he shook it. "It's short for Morni…" I was interrupted by a shriek. I pulled my hand back and looked to the side I heard it from.

"How could you do this to me on our month-aversary? It's a month ago today you asked me out and here you are with another girl." I looked up and saw a girl flying towards us. Could everybody here fly?

I leaned towards Dawn. "Is that Nora?" He nodded.

"I saw you, Dawn. You had your arms around her and were flying with her. We are over. I can't believe you'd do this to me."

"But…" Dawn started as Nora glowered form her high perch.

I spoke up. "We totally weren't, eww. It was a mix up. He thought I was you." She landed between us and spun around to Dawn, her hair flying in my face.

"You mixed *her* up with me?" Jutting her thumb back at me, she shook her head. "I don't care if you mixed up the sun and the moon, the dusk and the twilight, the morning and the dawn. Pardon the pun, honey." I laughed. "What's so funny?"

I held out my hand, "Let me introduce myself. I'm M. It's short for Morning. The pun you just used was double the pun-ness." Dawn's eyes twinkled as if he liked the joke, but was too afraid to laugh. I pulled my hand back.

"What's your last name?" He asked, stepping around Nora.

"Star. Morning Star."

"Well Dawn, it looks like you found your shining star. Your hunt is over and so are we." Her sarcastic tone pierced my heart. She was really angry. There were tears in her eyes and she sniffled. Suddenly she said, "Good-bye forever Dawn," And ran into the trees, disappearing from view.

"Arrrrg!" Dawn cried out. "Look what happened because of you!" He kicked a rock at me, but it missed. "I can't believe I mixed you up with my Nora, oh, my Nora." He stopped whining like a two year old and looked at me. "Hold up, did you say your name was Morning Star?"

"Y-Yes, is that a problem?" I stepped back. Mad men were not to be tampered with, I knew from experience with my father and brother.

"Duh! Because of you I just blew off my girlfriend!"

"Well I'm sorry, but I didn't exactly ask you to fly away with me. If I remember correctly, I wanted you to put me down!"

"Yea, well I didn't and now Nora's gone."

"I'm sure you'll see her again." I tried to sound comforting, but I had no idea how to comfort a grown boy, a man. Then I went over what had just been said…"Hold on a second! What did she mean about you finally finding me? Have you been looking?"

"In a way… yes. When I was born, an old man told my mother I would go on a quest for the morning star and travel with her to dangerous lands and learn what it truly meant to love. He said I would save her. But when my mom told me about it I thought the man must have meant the star in the heavens, not a… person."

"It still could mean the star in the heavens. I don't need your help in any quest and I think that last little rescue act was all the saving I need. Sorry, but I have to go." I started to walk off into the bush and my cell phone rang. Bleep! Bleep! … Bleep! Bleep!

"Hello?" I flipped it open, talking into the receiver.

"Hey, M." It was Anne. I didn't know I could get phone reception here in this new world.

"Anne! I am so glad to hear from you … No, I'm not at home. Why? … My house is burning? … How do you know? … Large smoke cloud? MmmHmmm … It's on the internet, too? Wow …" Then what I heard sank in. "Ahhhh!" After my scream, I fell on my knees and dropped the phone. I *had* to get home, *now!* There was talking on the other end and I picked up the phone again. "Yeah, Anne? I'm still here… I have to go, now. I'll be there as soon as I can. I promise… What? They think it was a bomb? … The fridge? … Oh my! I really have to go. Love you too, bye." I felt a hand on my shoulder and looked up. "Okay, I need your help now." I hung my head.

"Who was that?"

"Anne. She's a long time friend. She just called to tell me a bomb went off in my house and the billow of smoke is on the internet."

"Yup…" He looked at me strangely as I remained calm. "Is this a regular occurrence?"

"Is what?"

"Your house blowing up, you just told me and yet you seem so calm."

"Oh, yeah, that… MY HOUSE BLEW UP?" I gasped and fell over. "MY HOUSE BLEW UP! THAT'S NOT NORMAL! AHHHH!!" So much for remaining calm, I thought afterwards.

I started to cry. "It's okay…" Now Dawn was the one comforting me.

"No it's not okay. I'm lost in an alternate universe and my house is blown up. I have no way to get home, my parents will be so worried."

"Alternate universe? You're in Dovera, where do you want to be?"

"Earth."

"Earth? I've never met someone who *wanted* to go back there."

"Can you help? I got here through a garbage box in my back alley and ended up on a cliff. I was following an older man who said he was the son of the king here."

"The king we have now is a cruel, unjust ruler. He loves to set things on fire, just to watch them burn, and his fire is like Earth fire, it does a lot of damage. The trees are afraid of him. Have you met them, they are so nice. I can't believe anyone would burn them down for fun. The king is really mean. His only son is Sully. I really hate that guy. He thinks that, just because his dad has so much power over the kingdom, he's better than everybody. But, not to worry. He's a really bad fighter."

"I know. He also has terrible aim with a bow and arrow but somehow has perfect aim with a gun."

Dawn crouched by my side and looked at me in the face. "He's got a magic gun… Wait! You've met him?"

I sat up. "Yup. He tried to kill me, I got away. Followed him for a while, got stuck here. Old news."

"I wish you'd quit downsizing everything. He really is dangerous." He jabbed his hands into his pockets as his hair fell in his face. He flipped his head and it flew to the side in a wavy fashion. "So." He tried to start conversation again. "What did he try to kill you for?"

"Murder, treason, prison escape." I waited for his reaction, but he seemed to know I was kidding. I continued, "It totally would have made sense if he did it then, but he was trying to kill me for just being me." I spread out my arms for effect and made it so I had octopus arms. I pulled them back into my own, putting my hands in my lap. I sighed a big, defeated sigh. "I'm supposedly a 'beast'." I made quotation marks with my fingers.

"...A human that can change into all kinds of animals? Not just certain animal families? I've met dog people who can turn into all kinds of dogs, domestic and wild, and I've met cat people, but never a 'beast'! Sweet! You, Morning, are a very rare creature. You are a legend. Everyone has heard about the beast, but nobody has ever seen it... until now. People say it never changes in front of people and keeps to hi... ding..." He stopped when he looked at me. I had been changing different parts of my body, so that an arm would be one animal and an ear another and I kept changing until he noticed me.

"Boy! You talk like my brother at a comic book convention! I'm not a superhero, and does it look like I'm hiding it? Anyway, I can't be a legend! I am only eighteen!"

"Really? I'm twenty, almost twenty-one, and available." He wiggled an eyebrow.

I pushed his puffed out chest away. "No thank you. I really need to get going. Do you happen to know how to get back to Earth?" I stood up and brushed off my pants.

"No," he replied. I turned to walk away, he turned me back. "You didn't let me finish. No, I don't know how to get back to Earth, but I know someone who does. Follow me." And with that, he trudged off in the direction I had been going before.

I rolled my eyes and waited, but finally gave in and walked towards him. "Wait up!" I made myself a pigeon and flew at him. A dove soared down and tackled me. I casually grew a turtle shell and the bird made a snorting sound and flew away. I learned my lesson and walked to catch up with Dawn who had turned around waiting for me.

He did the eyebrow thing again. "I have a gift for you." He handed me a necklace with a tooth-like object on a thick string. I took it and felt it with the tip of my fingers. "It is the tip of a unicorn horn. Unicorns are said to be healers, as long as you are wearing it, you will be safe from all harm."

"Thank you, but I didn't acquire even a scratch from that little encounter." I pointed behind me to the eagle still flying away. "I am perfectly fine to take care of myself."

"Take it just in case. It would make me feel safer if you had it with you at least."

I rolled my eyes again. Since when did he care? "Fine." I stuffed it into my jeans pocket as we continued walking.

We walked in silence, and I could tell that Dawn was keeping his eye on me. "Hey, I kind of have a question to ask you. Do you have a boyfriend?"

"Um… no, but didn't you just have a girlfriend?" I quizzed back. The grin faded. He kicked at a rock.

"I never really liked her. My mom made me date her because she was the daughter of her best friend. She is so snobby and picky and nagged at me for everything. I sometimes wished I could move away from Dovera forever."

"What's Dovera?" We stopped for some apples. An apple tree was growing beside a river. It leaned towards us and dropped two apples into Dawn's hands. He said thank-you to the tree and handed an apple to me. We started to walk beside it on a little worn path.

"It's a world Canadian scientists found at the beginning of the earth time 1952. It has many doors that lead from your world to mine, but they are all contained in an 'Alberta'. Since then, they've sent people with powers and lug-nut wacko's here. Mrs. Bejweld, the woman I'm taking you to see, was one of the first to be banished here. It is an island with endless sea all around. We have nowhere to go, so we built our own world here. So Dovera is, in other words, where you are standing now."

"Right under my feet. But powers?" I felt my brow furrowing. "What? She was banished… I'm glad I didn't tell anyone important about my powers. Is everybody here been banished from earth?"

"At the beginning, it was just a place the Canadian government sent weird people, but we were magic and we could make our own government, our own world. Sometimes they sent their gone-wrong experiments here and we had to deal with them. Our current king was hit by some type of poisonous ray on Earth and now he's evil. We're still trying to get rid of him. He's horrible. I wish the people from your world never sent him. I was born here, and so was my mother, but my grandmother was the one who had been sent here. Many people you meet now will tell you second hand or third hand accounts of how awful Earth is, but few have been there. In some families, the original Earthling has passed on. My grandmother may have been dangerous in her day, but she's getting older now. Her 97th birthday was five days ago. The police on Earth probably still have her record." I sent a questioning look at him. "Telepathy. Her mind was too dangerous, I'm surprised they caught her at all."

"Oh! I've heard of her. Was your grandmother Mary Minder?" He nodded. "Funny nickname, always wondered about it myself. What about you? Did you inherit powers?"

"Yes, actually. From my dad's side; cold, fog and ice breathing, throwing and the ability to form snow, ice, and hail, also fog and rain in an instant. I don't like using my power. It scares even me. I also have ice vision." He stared at a dew drop on a tree leaf beside us and it froze instantly. He picked it up and handed it to me." I rolled it around in my finger as it slowly melted. You really ought to be careful of Sully, though, he has the power to sense power as well as the power to change his size. He could be listening to us right now, as a teeny tiny person, but never mind that. We have to get you to old Bejweld's house so you can go back to Earth and save your home from blowing up."

I looked at him. He was such a nice boy, even with his icy-laser vision. I still didn't know whether he accepted me with my animal morphing. "Thank-you. You know, your secret's safe with me." I turned into a wolf, a puppy, a lion, a bear, then back to myself. "Is mine safe with you?"

He gazed at me in bewilderment. "Yeah, but," He combed his hair with his hand. "You aren't safe from Sully; not when you keep changing out in the open like that."

"Isn't this a magical world? Can't I have magical powers and not be afraid? Plus I can take care of myself." He shook his head, hurried and I ran to catch up. Stopping at a ramshackle, spindly metal gate, he pointed.

"This is Mrs. Bejweld's home." I peeked inside. There was a large garden that had vines growing everywhere. The only way I could distinguish the house was by the window had stained glass in it that was shining through the greenery.

"Go save your home. If you ever come back, you'll look me up, right?"

"Yes."

"You are going to come back someday, right?"

"Yes."

"Do you like me?"

"Y-es."

"Can I kiss you?"

I stared at him in amazement. "Um… okay." I turned my head so he could kiss my cheek. He, instead, put one of his strong hands behind my head and tilted it up to kiss me on the lips. It was a sweet kiss and it lasted a long time, by my standards, and when it finally ended I stood there in dazed silence. He cocked his head and smiled at me; just watching my reaction to the kiss.

"I didn't know you meant the lips…" I stopped. He gave me a hug.

"That's okay, you are a pretty good kisser, but there's been better." He whispered in my ear.

"Hey…" I playfully hit him on the shoulder. "Anyway, thanks for all your help." I turned to wave. "And the kiss," I watched as he blushed. "Bye."

"Pleasure helping you, m'lady." He bowed and I laughed. I said good-bye one last time before turning towards the green estate. Pausing, I didn't know what to do. If I lived here, maybe we could be, but not when I was a world away. He really was a nice man. I waved once more and slinked as a weasel through the wrought-iron gate. I didn't become human again until Dawn had walked away.

Chapter V

Numbers 24:5-7 (NIV)

"How beautiful are your tents, O Jacob, your dwelling places, O Israel! Like valleys they spread out, like gardens beside a river, like aloes planted by the LORD, like cedars beside the waters. Water will flow from their buckets; their seed will have abundant water."

Wow, Dawn thought to himself as he walked away, Morning sure was something. Not just beautiful and athletic, but she had powers. He remembered her silky hair and how wonderful it had smelled when he was holding her. His arms felt like they belonged there, around her slender frame, like they should never let go. Even when he was telling 'Nora' it was okay, that he was there, he knew she wasn't Nora. She had spunk and personality that Nora lacked. She was smart, kind and honest and she had put her trust in him. He hoped Mrs. B really knew about the portal or he could be the bad guy in this fairy tale. He closed his eyes and saw her face, teasing him, angry at him, sympathizing with him. Who knew a girl could be pretty when she was mad? He saw her golden hair as it fell in her face. He longed to cup that face in his hands and stare at it all day and tell the person behind those beautiful honey eyes that he loved her, but who was he kidding? She would never think twice about a man who kidnapped her in a strange new world. She probably wouldn't even remember his name. He couldn't believe that so soon after Nora had dumped him he could fall in love, but he knew that the aching in his chest wouldn't go away until he saw her again. It wouldn't leave him until he had her in his arms. And that kiss... he had been lying to her when he said it was just okay. It was amazing. It sent a thrill through him he'd never felt before; A shiver up his spine, a tingling in his soul. She tasted like honey, warm and sweet. She was beautiful and cute and gorgeous, all at the same time. Too bad she wasn't his...

Subconsciously his feet had the same idea as his head did and he found himself jumping the fence around the property. He walked around and saw Morning striding around the house. Boy, she was pretty. She tucked a stray wisp of hair behind her ear and turned around. Her eyes seemed to look right through him and he felt his cold icy heart start to thaw. She was smiling and looking in wonder at all the different plants around her. He loved that smile. He sat down and contented himself with watching her. She even had a cute way of walking. He thought that over again; ***Boy, am I ever in love!***

☙

The place looked gorgeous. There were tall willows with branches hanging over small streams, and algae growing, giving the place a feel like it was a whole ecosystem. I saw something move in the corner of my eye, but it was just this really old willow with weeping branches hanging so low that behind them, around the trunk, would have been a perfect fort or hideout. I waved at the tree and the branches waved back. It was so cool that the trees were alive here. I took a whole 360 and simply looked. I walked around the tangled mass of plants in the middle that must have been the house. I wasn't looking where I was going when I tripped and fell.

My mouth full of dirt, I sat up and saw an old woman kneeling with her feet out behind her, and mine sprawled overtop.

"Meine Blumen sind herrlich. Sie sind eine Arbeit von Art. Stimmen Sie zu?" Asked the lady.

"Pardon, me. I didn't mean to trip over you. I'm really sorry." I apologised, I pulled my feet back, off hers. I slowly got into a sitting position.

"Oh, English. It's okay, young one. It brought no harm to me or my garden." For the first time, I really noticed the garden she was working on. It seemed lost with all the other plants and greenery around, but I could tell it was special. There were pink flowers and blue ones and purple, red and yellow ones. The blue one was shy but the yellow one waved. The pink one turned even pinker in a blush. There were tall flowers and short flowers and vines with bright blooms. I saw a hedge bordering it and a vegetable garden hidden underneath. "My flowers are wonderful. They are a workings of art. Do you agree, not?" I nodded, still looking. This place had a lot more vegetation than Earth did.

"They are gorgeous."

"May I help you? A favour did you come to ask of old Mrs. Bejweld, the lady with the green thumb?" She reached out and stroked a purple bloom. It leaned in to her touch like a cat.

"You do have a way with plants," I smiled at the flower, "And your garden really is lovely, but I did come to ask you a fav…"

"No figure of language used here, young one. I really have a thumb of green." I looked.

"Your power." I gasped in realization. "How were you banished from Earth for growing plants?"

She bowed her head in shame. "When I was little, I had fun making my vines alive. I would send them out to trip up kind people, I was mean and rude and hurtful to those who I loved most. The government found out and I had to pay my price. I was dragged to Alberta and sent here through a 'port hole' or something. But that's not what you really came to ask me, was it?"

"No." She put her trowel down and patted the dirt flat. Taking off her dirty gloves, she turned to me. "I wondered if you know how to get back to Earth. I'm from there and… I really want to get back." I stood up and brushed the dirt off my shirt, while peeking at her through the corner of my eye.

"What's the capital of Canada?" She quizzed.

"Ottawa."

"What's the capital of Mexico?"

"Um… Mexico?"

"Trick, it's Mexico *City*. What's the capital of China?"

"Hong-Kong, or is it Shanghai? Why are you asking me these questions?"

"I want to catch up. I miss being able to rattle off the forty-eight states of America and the twelve provinces and territories of Canada."

"There are fifty states in America. Alaska and Hawaii were added not too long ago and Canada has a new territory. Nunavut was split off of the Northwest territories in 1999."

"Oh, don't remind me I'm that old. Is it still 1999?"

"No, we're in the 21st century now. Its 2009, at least, it was when I left. That's why I came to you. I need to know how to get back to Earth. I want to go home."

Mrs. Bejweld looked around and came closer. "I know of a secret entrance to that world. I don't know where it will leave you, but it will take you back to your world. Follow me."

ᕦᕤ

Mrs. Bejweld toured me around her garden as she took the scenic route to wherever she was taking me. I decided after a bit to enjoy the scenery because it might make the trip worthwhile. Hopefully the entrance Mrs. B knew about wouldn't drop me off a cliff or in the middle of a river or anything. I began to wonder where it would lead me and if I could get back home soon. I crossed my fingers and hoped it wouldn't drop me too far North or in one of the mountain ranges. At least I knew that it was going to keep me in Alberta. I kind of hoped it would leave me close to home.

"Morning, dear-ie, this is favourite of all my ponds. This one is magic. You say what you want to see and it appears."

I started to pay attention again. "Can I try?"

"No. I don't let people see through it now-a-days. It's my own special secret in the back-forty of my property. Do they even say that on Earth anymore?"

"Only the cowboys and the entire state of Texas." She seemed pleased, and continued to walk, talking about the different plants and how she came to have them in her yard. I took one look into the pond and saw my reflection. It seemed like a normal pond. A dove appeared above my head. I spun around and the dove fluttered away. Was it the same one who attacked me earlier? I wondered. It was the only animal I had seen so far in Dovera.

Mrs. Bejweld walked ahead and I hurried to keep up. She was introducing the plants to me, and me to the plants. She seemed to be proud of me. The plants were friendly enough. Most of them smiled at me or were shy, a few came up and brushed my leg.

Soon we came to a fast winding river with a bridge below a small trickle of a waterfall. Mrs. Bejweld walked the opposite way from the bridge, away from the spraying falls. She took me to a huge tree that had one half of it's trunk on one side of the river and the other half on the other side. The two halves met at the top and made it so the roots formed a sort of door.

"Just walk through there and you will be home. Oh how I miss Earth."

"Thank you. Thank you very much." I walked towards the river and stepped in ten feet upriver from the waterfall. If someone was coming from the other side, they would need to be very careful of the water and the fast current. The water surged around my ankles as I turned and waved. I would never forget her friendship, or her kindness. I wished I could repay her in some way. "Thanks," I mouthed. I gave one of the trunks a pat before stepping in between the roots and disappearing from sight.

∽

When I stepped through the door to earth the sun was just rising, the same time as when I had left. I didn't know where I was, but at least I knew I was somewhere in Alberta.

I walked along the path I found and soon came to a busy street. It was one right outside of my community. Boy was I lucky. I raced along the street and up the drive to my house. But where my house should have been, only ashes remained. Anne was right, the bomb had gone off. I took out my cell phone and gave her a call.

"Hello?"

"Hi, Anne, I figured something out just now and I think you are in danger because you know my um... secret."

"Animal morphing? Yeah, I guess I know, but how am I in danger?"

"There's this man, he looks young, but I think he was way older than me, he blew up my house because he wanted my 'pelt' or something on his wall. He spoke of full moons and morphing, but it had to be my skin and I had to be dead." There was silence on the other end of the line. "Anne, you are my best friend and you've heard of superheroes and their families. The family is held for ransom until the hero will do what the bad guy wants. I don't want that to happen to you." I was walking and talking. In no time at all I was in front of her door. "Say yes, please, I couldn't bear it if you got hurt."

"Oh, alright."

"Good, open your front door and let's go." The door opened and Anne came out, already packed. I was confused. "Anne...?" I dropped the phone from my ear.

"I saw your house blow up and I heard the desperation in your voice on the phone last time, I packed already because I thought this might happen." She gave me a big smile. I stared at her and my cell phone gave me an extra loud dial tone to tell me I forgot to hang up. I flipped it closed. She walked out the door and placed her suitcase on the front step. "You aren't the only one with some sense in you." I laughed and picked up her suitcase. "Oh, and I told my parents that your family invited me on a cruise. I want them safe, too." We waved to Mrs. Walters and started off down the street. She came out at the last second.

"Anne, don't forget your cell phone."

"Um," I started, "There is no electronics allowed on the cruise so people can relax without having to worry about the world." Mrs. Walters put the phone on the windowsill and waved once more. I felt rotten to be lying to her, but if it kept her safe, it was worth it. She couldn't be able to contact us. Then she could honestly say she couldn't reach us.

We walked along in silence for a while when Anne asked a question that made me remember Dawn. She asked, "M, what's in your pocket, it is on a string, but is has an awkward shape."

I instantly remembered the unicorn horn and the healing and protection it was supposed to give. "Oh, *that*." I dug it out of my pocket and handed it to her. "It is a unicorn horn, well the tip at least. It is rumoured to be healing and give protection to the person wearing it." She smiled.

"Ooo! Like a force field around you that no one can penetrate! That is so cool!" She slipped it on over her head and fingered it lightly. "I can barely feel it. It's almost like it's not even there." She twirled it in her fingers once more before reaching around her neck to undo the knot that held it on. She struggled for a couple minutes before she asked if I could get it off. I looked at it. The knot was a mess it was all tangled and seemed impossible to untie.

"Um…" I stuttered, "That knot looks really complicated, how about you keep it on until we can find scissors to cut it off later."

She smiled. "I didn't know I could tie that complicated a knot that even you couldn't undo it. I will keep it on and safe for you, M."

I nodded and followed her to the bus stop. "I just really hope we don't need to use it."

Two blocks from the bus stop, we were still downtown and we soon found ourselves in a shopping crowd of tourists that appeared out of nowhere. We were jostled and pushed around as we battled our way through the mob. I saw someone elbow Anne in the chest and I lost sight of the necklace as it penetrated her skin. We hurried towards the bus stop and I left Anne sitting on the fountain as I got the tickets. When I came back out, I found Anne sitting on the fountain, right where I left her. Her suitcase was stuck between her legs and she was holding her chest, as if in pain.

I hurried over to her. "Are you oaky?" I asked. She was leaning over, in obvious pain, and then she sat up straight.

"I'm fine…" I looked where the horn tip had pierced her skin. It wasn't there, no scratch, no bump, no scar, no blood. You couldn't see it anywhere. It was as if she was healed instantly. Healed. That was it, the horn was supposed to heal the person who wore it, but where was the horn? The string hung loosely around her neck, nothing attached. It was nowhere to be found. Vanished. Maybe it dropped off after it pierced her skin… maybe, but not likely.

"Where is the horn?" I asked, starting to panic.

She stared at me and held her chest once again. "I think it's inside me."

Chapter VI

Jeremiah 30:12, 15a, 17a, 22 (NIV)

"This is what the LORD says: 'your wound is incurable, your injury beyond healing. Why do you cry out over your wound, your pain that has no cure? But I will restore you to health and heal your wounds,' declares the LORD. 'So you will be my people and I will be your God.'"

Mrs. Bejweld had watched the girl go. She was a beautiful young lady. Hopefully she found her way back home. There was a rustling in the brush and Bejweld froze.

"Who's there?" She yelled, but nobody responded. "I have ways of finding out." She rose her voice into the forest. The rustling continued, as if trying to get away. Mrs. Bejweld snapped her hand and the bush in front of her grew and caught a boy by the ankle with a vine, he was now hanging upside down in front of her. His back was to her for a few brief seconds, then he slowly started to spin.

"Hi, Mrs. B." It wasn't a boy, it was a grown man. It was her favourite young man, too. Mr. Dawn Starlight.

"Oops, sorry Dawn. Were you spying on me again?"

"No, I was just making sure my friend," He gulped and pointed to the roots and the river. "I was making sure she got home."

"So you were behind all of this, I should have known. Let's go back to the house, shall we? Have some tea and biscuits before that mother of yours starts looking for you." She let the bush drop Dawn and started to walk back to her house. "Follow me." Dawn rolled his eyes, so much for avoiding Mrs. Bejweld. It seemed that even the smallest difference in her forest was known about before it even happened. The lady really knew her garden, but it didn't help that the trees could tattle on him.

As he walked, Dawn wondered about Morning. He had given her the necklace, right? She couldn't be hurt now, but something didn't seem like it was supposed to be, he sensed that something had gone very wrong with it. Who was the friend Morning had been talking to on the phone? Alex? No, Andrea? No, Amanda? No, Anne? That was it! Anne. Something had gone wrong and Anne now had the unicorn horn. What was he thinking, of course

Morning wouldn't believe him about it. They had just met. But he thought she had trusted him…the more he thought about it, the less it seemed that the problem was planned, it had been an accident, he could feel it, but what could he do? He couldn't go traipsing into another world and just ask, 'Where's Morning? She has my magical unicorn horn'. That would be ridiculous! How could he save her? The answer hit him like a wave of nausea. He couldn't. He couldn't do anything to help her. She was on her own. He hung his head and followed after Mrs. B. Better to forget all about it since he couldn't do anything about it.

∾

"What?" I didn't mean to scream, but this was not what was supposed to happen. It was supposed to stay around her neck and protect her, not be driven into her skin and stay! "I'm so sorry, if I'd have known it was the least bit dangerous, I wouldn't have given it to you, honest!"

"That's ok M, you didn't know." She tilted her head down, trying to see it. "Is it bleeding?"

I looked again. "No."

"Is it there, can you see it?"

"No."

"It's all the way in?"

I nodded at her, "And it's already healed, too. Very odd."

"Very, I don't really know how to explain this to you, but I don't feel any hurt anymore, it went away."

"That's because it was meant to heal, but from the outside, though, not the inside…I don't think."

"Well, it's not bothering me, so let's continue on the trip as if nothing happened. And don't tell a soul. I kind of don't want it spreading around that I have a magical animal's horn imbedded in my chest."

I nodded, "Gotcha."

We walked to the bus in silence. Every once in a while I would glance over to make sure she was okay and I never saw so much as a twitch. The horn had disappeared and now it was in her, and I was going crazy! This couldn't be happening. I must be dreaming, just like I was dreaming about Dovera, but after a pinch, I came to the conclusion that this was real. All of this was real.

Getting on the bus, Anne went to sleep, but I couldn't. I couldn't stop thinking about how Dawn would feel if he knew that his necklace was inside my friend. Would he be mad?

40

Before noon, we switched busses, just outside of Calgary. I couldn't believe that with everything that happened, it wasn't even eleven o'clock yet. Talk about a long morning! We got on the bus and took the two seats closest to the front. I got the window, Anne got the aisle. I was planning on sleeping for the ride, but Anne had other plans, she was wide awake and wanted to hear all about my adventures in Dovera. I, personally didn't want to tell her, but when I mentioned a boy, rather man, who was very good looking, she wouldn't let me stop. Ugh! Girl gossip can give good info, but when you are the one gossiping, it is very tiring. It could be a full time job.

"Ooooo!" Anne's high pitched scream erupted when I told her he had kissed me on the lips in good-bye. "You didn't, yes you did! Eeep!" Now the driver was looking at us oddly. He had probably never witnessed girl talks, or squeaks, before. I started to bite my nails, this was getting embarrassing. Anne saw and grabbed my finger, "Stop that, it's gross." When she let go of my finger, though, my nail had no bite marks on it and it was all in one piece. I froze.

"Anne..." I whispered, still staring at my finger, "Anne?" She looked over and saw my finger. "What did you do?" She looked closer. "The nail," I hissed, "My nail is back to normal. What did you do?"

"I held your hand to stop you from biting and you didn't bite any more so I let go and now you are hissing at me. I think I might have healed you, though. Is that the kind of thing the horn tip was supposed to do?"

"AIRDRIE! Next stop Airdrie!" The bus driver boomed over the announcement system.

I looked at Anne, "Yeah, it was supposed to help heal, but I just don't understand why you can transfer the healing energy. Let's get off at the next stop, I'm going to try to fly to the lake."

❧

Anne and I stood up and told the driver to drop us off at the next stop. We got off and I changed into Pegasus so she and all her stuff could ride on my back. The flight was long and hard with lots of 'minor turbulence' and five Canadian geese in my horsey face. But, at last we arrived. I had been having some difficulty with landings, so I tried to gallop to a stop. As soon as my legs hit the ground, Anne and her things were thrown off my back and I was somersaulting along the ground, head over heels, mane over hooves. I gradually rolled to a stop in front of my parents, still a Pegasus. I groaned and flopped on my back, turning once more into myself. Racing out to see what the trouble was, they saw me with a wing just before I turned normal. They put one and one together and figured out that they were the ones who

41

made me animal. After that the whole story rolled out in front of them. I told them the parts that they didn't guess and saw the shock registering on their faces. They were mildly surprised but had partially already guessed my secret. Forgiving me for not telling them before, they agreed to help me find the man who tried to kidnap me and blew up our house. Then Seth sauntered in and I had to explain everything all over again. Anne filled in the parts I missed and that made three times that my story was told that day. I looked at the faces around me. These were the only people in my life who knew I had superhero powers. Those people included: Mom, Dad, Seth, and Anne. That was when I noticed Coco was missing.

"Where's Coco?" I asked.

"Oh," said Anne, "Your mom dropped her off at my house and my mom will take care of her until our 'cruise' is over."

I nodded at them, "That was a very wise thing to do." We all went inside and had some hot chocolate, my favourite feel-better drink in the world. Soon we were all ready to talk about what we were going to do.

I had gathered everyone here for one reason only, ok maybe two. One: They were here so they were safe. Whoever was trying to get me would stop at nothing to get me, even hurt those who knew my secret. Two: They were the only ones who could help me stop whoever was trying to get me. We chose the cottage at the lake, I guess, because we no longer had a house and didn't want to endanger Anne's parents.

I told my mom, dad and brother about the portal to the magical world. I told them all about my adventure, minus the kiss this time, I had learned my lesson with Anne. I also told them that I had befriended an old lady who also knew my secret and that most people in Dovera had some type of superpower. Telling them about the house blowing up and the boy who wanted my skin made them screech and cringe. Seth was amazed I had survived. He was almost… proud of me? Odd, well, odd for Seth at least. He also seemed kind of interested when Anne mentioned she wanted a boyfriend. I guess she was a little jealous of Dawn. Who knew a mangy old brother would care if your best friend had a date or not?

After my story, my family wanted to know what Dovera looked like. I told them that Dovera is a lot smaller than Canada, almost the size of Vancouver Island, maybe a little bigger. "It could be compared to Scotland." I said, "Like Scotland it has many hills, and green scenery. The sunsets are gorgeous and magnificent. The rivers and streams are fresh and clean. The streets were clear of litter." I also told them that it wasn't an island as far as I knew. It had the cliff thing that seemed to be the end of the world, well the desert on the other side of the cliff seemed to go on forever, but I doubted you could actually go there. Maybe there was another world attached if you went further on, but I hadn't found it. Two days later, school ended and Anne and I graduated high-school, my parents asked if there was a way to get to Dovera. I said yes and they went wild. They were so excited and wanted me to show them Dovera so we got ready and went back to the portal I had taken from Mrs. Bejweld's. I showed them to the secret entrance and told them about the river. We decided to wear raincoats and bring all our belongings in knapsacks. I warned them how high the water was and we stepped through the portal to Dovera.

My mother went through first and even when she stepped through we could still hear her scream. I guess the water level went up since I was last there. I stepped through and screamed. The place wasn't anything like it was before. It was full of weeds and vines were overgrown. There was no room to walk, no room to move. I asked the vines to move, but they didn't speak. They didn't move. I pulled at some of them and heard the tree speak.

"Hey, there, let me help you. Someone tangled these stupid things around my trunk and I didn't have the guts to take them off." Long branches reached down and pulled the vines away so my family could walk through. Anne was stunned; she hadn't really believed there were talking trees in Dovera; neither had Mom because she screamed when the tree talked to her.

"Thank you." I said to the tree. I shook it's branch and started to walk off. My family were still staring at the tree.

"Can you really move?" Anne asked.

"Yes," replied the tree, "But not very far. I am a portal to another world. I have to stay put. Other trees you may come across love to move; but my roots like the soil they're in, plenty of water, and my leaves love the part of sky they're in, plenty of sunlight, so I am happy to stay put." Anne nodded, still getting used to the idea that she was talking to a tree.

"Wow."

"Yes, it is quite amazing, young one," answered the tree, "But you must be off. I think your female leader wants to get moving."

"Yes I do." I answered back. "Anne, if you loved the talking trees, wait 'till you meet the flowers!" She giggled and became all excited which meant she was happy and couldn't wait to meet the blooming beauties.

I was still a little irked that somebody learned about my visit a while back and had pulled a trap to stop me, too bad it hadn't worked. I made sure that everyone was present and accounted for and we trekked through the neatly trimmed forest towards Mrs. Bejweld's house. I looked back one last time, and from my angle, it looked like an artist had tried to creatively 'tie-up' the portal so that nobody could get in or out. It gave me the creeps to think of who I was dealing with. I shivered and turned to face my comrades, they were trusting me to lead them to victory and that is exactly what I was planning to do... after a quick visit to Mrs. Bejweld's house, that is.

છ૭

Mrs. Bejweld, the kind old lady who took us in, was short and stout. She had a plump jolly face with rosy cheeks and dimples. Her olive green eyes twinkled and beamed when she smiled. She was getting old but her thin wispy grey hair was still long and in a thin braid wrapped tightly in a fat bun. Her small cottage was warm, cozy and comforting, with the small fire flickering happily in the fireplace. The shadows danced across the walls to a tune of the magical world. The one different thing from Dovera to Earth is the fire warms but doesn't burn to the touch. It doesn't smoke or need fuel to burn, it's magic! Other than that, Mrs. Bejweld and her home were normal and not magical.

The small pond near her cottage though was very magical. It was a looking mirror to whatever you wanted to see in any realm or world. When Mrs. Bejweld showed it to us, Anne went first and asked to see her parents. Her mom was asleep on her bed with droops under her eyes like she had slept for days. Her father was up washing dishes and was almost asleep on his feet. I wonder what had kept them up. Maybe they just missed Anne so much. I hated to see them like that, but I had to look for Anne's sake. She started to cry, and I put a comforting arm around her. My mother went next. She asked to see our old house—or at least the remainder of it. She saw a pile of debris and burning fires all around. Then she saw construction vehicles and cranes. They were going to turn our house into condos or apartments! Mom nearly cried, too but she held back and only gave a whimper of disapproval and surprise. Dad passed up his turn; he said all he wanted to see was his family and friends safe and sound. He gave us a hug and I was glad for the reassurance.

Seth passed up his turn also, but I leaped at the chance, Mrs. Bejweld didn't offer often. I thought slowly and knew within minutes what I wanted to see. I wanted to see the ones who were behind all my attacks and the bombing of our house. The picture that followed was fuzzy and hazy. It was in black-and-white verses the colour images that the others had seen. I could see two distinct shapes. One was short and skinny and, the other was tall and fat. The first was arguing to the second and the second kept shaking his head. I asked Mrs. Bejweld why it was hard to see when Anne and mom's pictures were so clear. She replied that the pictures lose their colours when they are showing something in Dovera and that it turns fuzzy if they were evil. There was no doubt about it that whoever was after me was evil and had no heart.

I had to find him but the picture didn't give me much information that I didn't already know. Now I knew that there were two, or that there was a sidekick of some sort. I knew one had to be the boy, but both looked so different, I couldn't tell which was him. I knew now that they were somewhere in Dovera, but not necessarily near Mrs. Bejweld's home. I also knew they were fighting over something of great importance. I looked back at the picture. It was still hazy but all of a sudden the short skinny one saw us and pointed us out to the tall fat one. I saw him mouth the word 'Dad'. The 'Dad' looked at me, his cold icy grey-fuzzy eyes dug into my heart with hate. He looked in my eyes and then nodded. Soon after the pond went blacker than ink. I heard Mrs. Bejweld behind me gasp.

"What's wrong?" I couldn't keep the panic out of my voice. She said she had never ever seen the one who was being looked at look at us before and never before had the pond gone ink black.

Something was wrong.

They knew we were here.

But the only question on my mind was: who were 'they'?

Chapter VII

You Are my All in All: by Dennis Jernigan

"When I fall down you pick me up; when I am dry
you fill my cup; you are my all in all."

I thought about it for a long time and sat on the edge of the pond. The tall fatherly man seemed in charge, while the shorter one seemed to jump to conclusions. I fell asleep that night from exhaustion and weariness. I couldn't stop myself from thinking about the short man who had seen me. I could have sworn I'd seen him before, but I couldn't remember when or who he was. I had seen those ragged features before and that same icy stare. It was like I was in a dream and I was just waking up after a long sleep but couldn't remember what had happened. Who was he? Could he possibly be the man who wanted me dead? I asked around the breakfast table the next morning, but my family was too interested in the appearing food and disappearing dishes. They just thought about what they wanted for breakfast and it appeared. And no one had to do the dishes! They just disappeared when you were done with them. It was so fascinating that I was completely ignored. I felt anger rush inside me; we were here to catch a crook, not on vacation! But looking at Anne and Seth's joyful faces all the anger rushed out as quickly as it had rushed in. My family was safe and happy, that was all that mattered. We would take one rest day and continue our journey tomorrow. I was so sleepy, which was partially from the warm meal in my satisfied stomach and partially from exhaustion and from the amount of sleep I got last night, which was little to none. The face of the wicked man would not leave my mind. It was as if it was burned in my head, behind my eyelids.

On our vacation day we toured Rosette, the little town that was close by to Mrs. Bejweld's house. Mrs. Bejweld then introduced us to one of her best friends, Ms. Dellux. Dellux was the teacher at the one room school house in Rosette. In it were three grades, one, five and eight, and seven students. Three were in grade one, two in grade five and two in grade eight. She was Mrs. Bejweld's foil in so many ways. Bejweld was short and fat. Dellux was tall and thin. Bejweld was old and had greying hair and rosy cheeks. Dellux was relatively young and had carrot red hair and pale features. Her skin had no marks at all while Bejweld had freckles and a scar above her right eye. Bejweld had loving, kind olive green eyes, while Dellux had cold uncaring black eyes that I would describe as beady. Her clothes looked new and ironed and she was a sanitary freak, yes, freak. She would not shake my hand and wore gloves when she had to touch anything that wasn't her own.

I felt twitchy around her. Call it bad vibes or animal instinct but I felt that she was trying to see though me to my secret and beyond, but not really caring about what she found. I later told Anne and even though she has no animal powers, she felt the same about Ms. Dellux. I felt that she was not quite evil, that word may have been too strong, but maybe loosely wound in the large problem that was my life. She could be trusted, but with little, and definitely not with my secret.

A while back, when Mrs. Bejweld had found out my secret, I had told her to keep it secret no matter what. I told her that she couldn't tell a soul. Now I asked if she had told Ms. Dellux. She replied warily that she had very much wanted to but hadn't because of her promise to me. I told her I was thankful and that the promise was still intact, even more so now that I was actually in Dovera.

For the rest of our vacation day we experimented with magic in various stores. The general store was first. As soon as we stepped in we felt the pleasure and cheerfulness of the place. There were no shelves because all the goods floated. Whatever you wanted most just floated up to you. A small oven mitt with butterflies floated up to Mom, along with necklaces and other jewellery that hooked all over her. Seth was pummelled with gumballs and candy, but they stayed afloat. He soon got used to it and held his mouth open. Anne was nearly knocked over by a new bike. It was red and silver with a red helmet to go with it. It was an 18 gear mountain bike. She got on and started pedaling through the air. Dad was dodging drills and saws and fishing rods that threw themselves at him, while the newest fashions tried him on for size and golf clubs put themselves in his hands. I just stared and smiled. A length of rope slid into my belt and spying glasses wiggled on my ears. I was surprised that anything would find me, but I guess I would need the items in the future. A horse saddle told me I would be horsing around with my family soon. A slingshot flipped into my backpack. I just stood still and the various items attached them onto me where they would need to be for the future. A hat was placed on my head. What was that for? Many different CD's, attached together by an elastic were flown into my pack. A flashlight zoomed in just as I was zipping up the zipper on the backpack. Then we paid for the merchandise, with the emergency money from the emergency backpack I had brought from Calgary, and left for the bakery. As we were leaving I found a secret compartment in the hat. *I wonder what that's for…* I thought. But, knowing our circumstances, I would find out soon enough.

The bakery was almost as amazing as the general store, the smells were sweet and warm and I could see the bread rising in the ovens. The food floated on pink napkins and had icing sugar sprinkled over the top. We each got one treat and then headed back to Mrs. Bejweld's.

The walk back to Mrs. Bejweld's cottage after the visit to the bakery was relaxing and gorgeous. We took a well worn trail, which had been used many generations before. We were surrounded by trees. Some were still blooming and some were bundles of leafy greens. All waved and giggled and sang to us as we passed by. The smell was sweet and distinct. No change between Earth and Dovera's tree blossoms, except for the dancing. We came across an apple tree and a small stream. There Mrs. Bejweld decided we should settle down for lunch. I remembered that I passed a tree like this one when Dawn was taking me to Mrs. Bejweld's house the first time. The tree kept dropping apples for us as long as we could eat them. Seth and Dad ate their fill of apples, maybe seven or eight, but Anne, Mom and I only ate two each. By the time we were finished, the sun was at its highest in the sky and the shade under the apple tree advertized luxurious sleep in the cool shade. It moved its branches so the sun only peeked through, but not enough to make the spot warm; it was very kind of the apple tree. The old cobblestone bridge was in view from the chosen hiding spot. While the adults slept, the kids played.

I know we were beyond 'kid' age but that's how we acted at the stream. It all started when Seth found a large, round, smooth stone. He decided to show off to us girls how far he could skip it. He jumped on the rimmed edge of the bridge and prepared to throw. I glanced at the adults: good, they were asleep and couldn't interfere with our fun. I jumped on the railing and Anne soon after did the same.

He skipped it and it went five skips before plonking into the river. He hopped down and picked up four more rocks. None got over six skips. On the last rock, I asked him a question.

"You haven't done so well. Do you think you could get seven skips?"
"Yes!"

"I don't think so. I bet you five dollars you can't skip that," I nodded at the rock, "seven skips." Anne wobbled on the bridge and Seth reached out an arm to steady her.

He turned back to me. "I can and will" He retorted.

"Nuh-uh! No, you can't, not in a million years!" I stepped closer. He flicked his wrist and the rock went flying. It hit the water once and started to bounce. One…two…three, four. *Oh, no,* I thought, *he might actually make it.*

He sneered at me, thinking the same thing. Five…six…*Eeeep*, I panicked and used magic to make the stone fall in mid-bounce.

A fish jumped out of the water and bumped it. To an ordinary person, it looked like an accident, but I really asked the fish to bump the rock, and yes, I'll admit it, I am a sore loser.

"Oh, too bad. That really is rotten luck." Anne said.

I heard Seth growl. He obviously didn't think it was a coincidence.

"Morning you cheated!" His yell echoed around the bridge. He turned and pointed a finger at me.

I glanced at the adults. They were still sleeping. How could they still be sleeping with Seth's loud voice?

He stepped closer. "You," He made a push at me. I heard Anne in the background yell 'No!' and from then on life went in slow-motion. Each movement in its own frame, it felt like it took five minutes, when it really only took a few seconds.

Frame 1: Seth's arms flail out in aggravation at me.

Frame 2: I feel a burning in my chest.

Frame 3: Seth's eyes grow wide.

Frame 4: I felt my feet slip off the wall and reached out to grab the rail. Seth reaches out to grab me back.

My right arm scrapes the rock and the freezing cold water touches my toes.

Then it's all around me; I feel stones beneath my sore, cold body.

I feel one large stone bump me on the head.

And then, like the pond, everything went black.

The last thing I remembered was Anne's scream of horror.

༼༽

Morning was out cold, literally cold, and floating down river. Anne screamed and reached out to hit Seth but he was faster. He grabbed her wrists and held her shaking struggling body tight until she calmed down. Then he jumped off the wall, pulling her after him.

He soothed, "She'll be okay, let's go. Don't wake mom and the others with screams. We can do this without them."

She pulled away from his tight grasp. "You did this to her! Over five dollars!" Anne started to cry. "I hate you Seth! I hate you!" She pounded her fists on his chest in agony and with that she ran down the bank after Morning.

Her words stung more than her hits, but why? Why should he care whether his sister's friend hated him or not? But in his heart, he knew he cared because he liked her… maybe… just a little… but he'd never tell Anne, or Morning. Seth followed, keeping his distance so he didn't accidentally overcome her and make her angrier. Boy did Morning ever pick some loyal friends. Anne finally got tired and stopped running to walk fast, scanning the banks to see if Morning washed ashore. Seth slowly walked up beside her.

"If you had just given her some warning…" She let her sentence hang. That way it was more devastating.

He jabbed his hands in his pockets. "Ok, Anne, look, I'm sorry. If I'd have known what would happen, I wouldn't have. I was mad because she cheated." He turned his head to look at Anne, only to get a smack in the face.

"You doofus!" Anne screamed. "We are in Dovera. A *magical* world! Morning using magic in a magical world is like using a stove in a cooking competition! She had every right and it was only five bucks!" The thought struck him like another one of Anne's smacks. She was every bit right. He decided to change the subject.

"So what happens when the Bejweld lady and Dad and Mom wake up to find us all gone? Did you ever think of that before running away?" He thought he'd stumped her, but no, Anne had an answer for everything.

"Yes, Seth, I have." Her voice was calmer than she felt. "They will think something came up and M had to take us somewhere safer. They won't worry for a few days. Morning's been here before and knows the area, they will think we were attacked and had to run." Again, she was every bit right.

The pair had walked along in silence for a bit when they heard a voice. "Come on fishy-fishy. Come to papa. I want my supper, little fishy." It was an old croaky voice. Seth pulled Anne behind a large willow, whose long branches hung around them like a curtain. He slowly turned and peeked around the tree.

"Why hello," the tree started to say, but Seth shushed it. In the clearing by the stream was an old man with a long fishing rod, talking to a large trout he was trying to reel in. There was an empty metal bucket beside him for the fish. Also, there was a small can dated 1952 with a wriggling mass of worms in it. Seth felt Anne behind him slide uncomfortably at the sight of them.

He turned around and asked her, "So… do we talk to him?"

"Of course we do!" Her answer was simple and Seth couldn't argue. "If you ever want to find your sister we have to take chances. Unless we missed her back a ways she floated right past this old geezer and he can tell us if she had woken up, or if she is still floating away downriver." Seth thought for a while.

"I guess," He started, "But remember we are in magic world, he must know magic! If Morning knew magic and she's from Earth, then he must because he is from…" He watched her run to the old man. Rats! She wasn't listening, but then, neither did Morning.

"She's pretty." The tree whispered, parting its branches to look at her as she talked to the old man.

"Put those back!" Seth exclaimed, "They're hiding me!"

"Why hide from a beautiful girl like that?"

"No," Seth whispered in aggravation, "Not the girl! I'm hiding from the man!" The tree was silent and Seth watched and waited, reading Anne's actions like a book. She pointed at the river and then made herself look like Morning had and the old man nodded and held up a two on his fingers and put his hand over his eyes and looked over the river. Finally Anne said something and pointed to the tree where Seth was still hiding. He wasn't a people person. Why was she pointing him out? The old man dropped his fishing rod and followed Anne back to the tree.

"Seth, Seth, where are you?" She asked.

"He's over here." The tree said, pushing Seth out from behind its trunk with a few fragrant blossoms. He gave the tree a frown and turned to Anne and the old man.

"Thanks," Anne said to the tree, "Seth, this is Mr. Yetton. He saw Morning and spent two hours trying to get her. He said the water was trying to keep her away from him. He finally got her out of the water and she is back at his cottage. Isn't that awesome?" Her voice was excited. He should be happy but he felt that something was wrong still.

"Was there anything wrong with her?" Seth asked Mr. Yetton. He saw the slight bob of the old mans head.

"Yes, I'm a sorry to say that ye wee young lass has yet to awake from her deep dreams." Mr. Yetton's accent could be described as Scottish or Irish on Earth. He rolled his R's and had a voice gravely like he was speaking through his throat. He walked with an oak cane and mumbled as he hobbled, his bony knees looked like they could cave under the pressure of his body at any moment. His clothes were patched and ragged with well-worn plaid patterns on them and a straw hillbilly hat was positioned crookedly on his nearly bald head. His long white beard and pale blue eyes showed years of wisdom.

"Wow that must have been a pretty hard bonk on her head she got if she's still out cold." Anne replied. "Can you take us to her Mr. Yetton?" Her innocent voice cut through the silence.

"Nay, ye young lass an' laddie, ye friend needs her rest. Come on a back tomorrow an' we'll see." Mr. Yetton's voice was kind but firm when he said this, as not to be argued with. After that he turned and walked back to his rod and continued fishing. Anne stood wide-eyed, gaping, almost at the point of tears. She took a step towards the retreating old man, and then decided against it.

She turned to Seth. "So, now Mr. bright ideas what do we do now?" Her hands were on her hips as she prodded further. "If you wouldn't have pushed her then we wouldn't be in this predicament! We are so close and yet so far. Where do we sleep tonight?" She was almost yelling.

"Keep that up and follow me. Get quieter as we walk." His whisper told her he had an idea. She looked and saw Mr. Yetton trudge off with his fishing gear.

"So what's your bright idea this time Seth." She started, "You've made a mess of everything. Where are we going to sleep? What are we going to eat? What happens when Mrs. Bejweld and Mr. and Mrs. Star wake up to find us gone? Seth…" She had done as she was told. She had rambled on and had gotten quieter and quieter as they walked further into the woods. Soon they came across a cabin nestled deep in the trees, with a large tree and a well beside it. Seth had followed the old Mr. Yetton right to his cottage. They would sleep outside it for the night and intrude in the morning.

They would rescue M at the first light of dawn. Anne laughed thinking about the man M had met last time she was in Dovera. Dawn. What a funny pun.

Chapter VIII

2 Timothy 1:7 _(NKJ)
"For God has not given us the spirit of fear, but of
power and love and of a sound mind."

As soon as I woke up the one thing I noticed was that my head hurt, and I was cold. I slowly peeked open my eyes. All around me was unfamiliar objects. There was a man and a woman. They were arguing about me. Who were they? My parents? They must be and I must be in my bed. I tried to move my arms and legs to get up. I managed a sitting position with lots of aches and pains. They noticed me and raced over to help.

"I don't think you should try to get up yet, young Evening." The man, my father, advised me.

"Where am I?" It took a while to form the words, but I got them out. My mouth felt like jelly, wiggling and wobbling about, it made the words sound very slurred. "My head hurts." I gave up trying to sit up and laid back down in hopes for the stinging headache to go away. I closed my eyes and the dizziness slowly left me thinking that the world really did spin. Maybe dad was right, I shouldn't try to get up yet. The light from the window was wobbling and twisting in patterns that I couldn't think of. All of a sudden, I saw the light take the form of a dove. It smiled and I blinked to make sure it was there. Why was it there?

"You were playing with a bunch of your friends and fell off the bridge, dear." I twisted my head around from the dove to the adults. A tall, slender woman with black eyes was talking. That must be mother. I closed my eyes once more. I needed more sleep and headache pills; it must've been some fall. My eyelids were scratchy and my mouth dry, but I didn't have the effort to raise an arm or ask for help. Speaking of arm, my right arm throbbed. It was a searing pain that I could feel my heartbeat in. *What happened?* I thought.

I squeezed my eyes shut, thinking that if I drifted off into a dreamless sleep, things would look better later, and they might even stop spinning.

Before I dozed off, though, I heard dad say in a whisper to mom: 'It's working just fine'. I thought to myself that he must mean the medicine then I fell into a black hole of no pain.

❧

As soon as Mrs. Star woke she felt something out of place. Where were the kids? Were they attacked again? Were they ok? She had to get back to Mrs. Bejweld's cottage to take another look in the pond. She looked at her husband. He looked so peaceful when he slept. Did she really want to wake him? But there was no choice. She had to. Her children's lives depended on it. She put a light hand on his shoulder and gently shook him. In a soft calm voice she said, "Dear, come on dear. Wake up Nate. Nathan…" She shook again. "Honey, wake up."

He made a gurgling noise and sleepily replied, "In a minute, sweet-ums." He turned his head and put one of his large callused hands on her small soft one.

Amy pulled her hand away, startling Mr. Star. "No Nathan, now! The kids may be in danger." Her voice was strong and powerful, with a sense of authority. He woke with a start and busied himself trying to get his stiff muscles to cooperate. Amy then went over to Mrs. Bejweld, who was also waking up. "Mrs. Bejweld, we need to take another look in the pond, the kids are missing." Even though they were eighteen and twenty, she still referred to them as 'kids'.

Mrs. Bejweld nodded and got up with surprising speed. She put her shoes back on, grabbed Mr. and Mrs. Star's hands and led them across the cobblestone bridge at a quick walk. Amy was looking at the bridge and saw a scrape of blood on the railing and a tear of Anne's clothing downstream on a bush. Mrs. Bejweld rushed them along before Amy could take time to wonder what had happened. Their fast pace made up for lost time. A usual half hour's walk was traded for a thirteen minute run. They reached the pond with amazing speed and Mrs. Star asked to see her daughter.

A black-and-white picture showed up two seconds later. Good, so she's still in Dovera, Amy thought. She looked closer. Morning was lying on a bed in an unfamiliar cottage. She had scrapes and bruises all over everywhere, but it was still Morning. Beside the bed were two fuzzy figures. Great, she's been caught by the evil side, Mrs. Star thought. Again, she heard Mrs. Bejweld gasp. Amy turned around to ask her what was wrong when she saw the old woman's finger pointing at the picture.

"Delly, that's Ms. Dellux!" The young woman they had met in town that day was fuzzy and black-and-white but being her best friend, Mrs. Bejweld had recognized her instantly.

"So she's on the ugly side, now, is she?" Mrs. Star had gently asked. Bejweld stuttered her reply.

"I-I-I did-did-didn't know, h-h-honest!" The older lady had tears in her eyes. "I didn't know she would capture little Morning."

"It's ok, it'll be ok." Nate finally decided to speak up. "Let's see Anne and Seth next." The pond rippled, like a stone had been thrown in its centre and flicked to Seth and Anne. They were up a tree looking at a cottage. It was the same cottage Morning was being held prisoner in! They were talking and also black-and-white. So all the kids were still in Dovera, and Morning had been captured by an evil man and Ms. Dellux, and Seth and Anne were going to try to save her. They had to get to the cottage! And they had to get there fast!

℘

The tree they finally decided to sleep in was uncomfortable. Branches were sticking this way and that and poking into her backside. Anne had tried rolling over but almost fell out of the tree. The tree had tried to catch her, but only made her fall farther.

"Trees weren't made for sleeping. We aren't very comfortable," it had said. Seth seemed comfortable enough. But his mind wasn't on the tree; it was on the events of the day. He had nightmares every time he closed his eyes; he could see his little sister falling…falling…out of reach…gone. He'd see her face as he pushed her. He'd see her eyes grow wide and her arms flail out to grab onto the railing, but with every prayer he prayed she still fell into the swirling black rapids over and over in his mind. She fell into the river, washed away and was in this cottage recovering at the moment with a very protective old Mr. Yetton not letting them see her. He felt that it was all his fault. He only hoped Morning was alright. He looked at the glow-in-the-dark watch he was wearing. It was M's. It was also one o'clock in the morning. He should be asleep by now.

All of a sudden he heard voices coming from the cottage, and the kitchen light turned on. It was blinding in the night for a few brief seconds. Seth almost lost his balance, but grabbed a branch that moved closer to help steady himself. He knocked himself on the head, how stupid for him to forget he was in a tree. Soon his eyes became accustomed to the light, just like they had become accustomed to the dark. He saw the man wandering about by the window, his shadow casting a rippling black form on the curtain. Soon a woman joined him. Wait! Was it? Could it be… no, it couldn't be, but it was. The woman at the window was none other than Ms. Dellux, Bejweld's really odd friend that Morning had been so uncomfortable with earlier when they were all touring Rosette. That tour seemed years ago but it was really only yesterday afternoon. Wow, so much had changed since then. He turned around awkwardly in the tree and swung over to Anne. She looked so peaceful in sleep, should he wake her up? She had had a long day and needed her rest, but she was Morning's best friend. *Anne is a better friend to Morning than I am*, he thought sourly. But then Anne would never push M off a bridge because she lost a bet. He never thought he would, either, but now look where they were. He paused, hand above her shoulder. She stirred and tried, desperately to roll over, her hands out as if to stop something from falling. She was having nightmares, too and it was his fault. It was *all* his fault. If he hadn't pushed her, they would be back at Mrs. Bejweld's house asleep in normal beds and resting for the journey to the bad guy's lair later that day. *Well,* he thought to himself, *we are one day ahead of schedule.* He rested his hand gently on Anne's shoulder and shook her. She sat up instantly and almost bonked her head on his.

"W-w-w-what, I-I'm awake…I think. W-w-what's wrong?" Her sleepy voice was music to his ears. She was okay, at least. He had to keep her safe and get his sister back.

"They're moving around in the cabin. Our raid may not be able to wait until dawn." She nodded, and tried to get up. She had forgotten they were in a tree and her foot slipped.

"Help!" Her low whisper told him she was still half-asleep and thought she was falling off the bridge.

"Shh, we have to be quiet, I've got you." Putting his arms around her, he shook her awake. Wow, was she ever light. He heard her mumble something and then she was on her feet.

"I'm okay," She swerved dizzily and then shook her head, stood up straight and looked at Seth. "We have to get down and get a closer look. What could they possibly be doing at…" She grabbed Seth's watch, "One in the morning?" Taking a huge risk in the dark, Anne jumped, or rather hurled herself down to a branch two feet below them and eight feet from the ground. She dropped and motioned for him to follow. Gymnastics was never his sport. He was never good at jumping, and he wasn't too keen on heights, either.

"If you wouldn't mind, dear tree, can you lift me in one of your branches and put me on the ground?"

"No, you must do it on your own, plus, I can't see in the dark and might hurt you."

"Right." Seth said and then he jumped, not for Anne, or for himself, but for M. He had to get his sister back. Well that was what he thought before he landed hard on one ankle and twisted it. Then he decided he'd better give up.

"No way!" Scream-whispered Anne. "You will not give up! I will make you go on until you save her or else…"

Seth smiled. "Or else what?"

"I will have to hit you."

Yeah, like that was going to happen, EVER. He gave a snicker.

She touched his ankle and it was magically all better. All healed.

"Are you ready now, slow poke?"

"Huh," was all he managed, bewildered that the pain had gone so quick.

"What?" He mumbled before he was dragged by the wrist to the cottage.

Chapter IX

Psalm 38:5, 20-22 _(NKJV)

"My wounds are foul and festering because of my foolishness. Those who render evil for good, they are my adversaries, because I follow what is good. Do not forsake me, O LORD; O my God, be not far from me! Make haste to help me, O LORD, my salvation!"

I had slept for hours when I finally awoke at midnight. The house was dark and my room seemed unfamiliar. No wonder. I had fallen off the bridge and bonked my head, hard! I would probably be unfamiliar with things until my memory returned. I stumbled around the house until I found mom's room. The covers had been thrown back but she wasn't there. I went on, looking for Dad. I found them both in the kitchen, having a cup of coffee.

"Hi, I couldn't sleep." I was very awake.

"Come here, Evening." I came obediently. So, my name was Evening. Wow that must have been a hard bonk, I didn't even remember that; it seemed so unfamiliar. My feet seemed like lead as I stumbled over to mom.

"What, mom?" I asked hesitantly. "Did anyone else fall in the river?" I hoped they weren't going through what I was going through. My head started to spin. I wobbled, and then steadied myself.

"No, dear, but your uncle and I have decided we need someone else to help take care of you. You've run wild these last few years and you need some discipline." Her voice was monotone. I couldn't tell whether she was happy or sad that I was to leave. And the man was my uncle, not my dad. I must have hit my head harder than I thought. "We're going to ban you from leaving the house until we're packed." Ban. That triggered a memory. Anne. I saw a flash of blonde hair and blue eyes. She must be one of the friends I'd never see again.

"Where will we be moving to?" A lump clogged my throat. I hoped it was somewhere I'd like.

"Your cousin in Waterloo, you remember him? Oh, and you should remember his father, the king of Dovera." Dellux knew she wouldn't, this was all a scheme to turn her light to dark; her good to go sour; the animal-whisperer to evil.

"Dovera? Uh…no, I kind of don't remember that much." I lowered my head, hoping to stop the blazing headache. "My head hurts." I cradled my throbbing head in my hands. "Owwww," I moaned and saw a flicker of a smile twitch mom's lips as if she wanted me to forget my entire life. As if she wanted me to suffer pain. I guess it was my punishment for running off. She really didn't think I'd do it again like this, did she? "I'll go get my things." I saw mom flash her icy black eyes. Where had I seen that before? *Probably before I hit my head, and every single day of my life,* I thought. How long was my life, anyway, how old was I? "How old am I? I seem to have forgotten."

They both ignored me and went to their rooms to pack. Something felt wrong. A twist in my gut told me they weren't who they seemed. But who were they? I just couldn't remember.

And my head hurt.

"Dear, Mrs. Bejweld, do you happen to know that cottage?" Mrs. Star was in a rush. What dreadful things could happen to her kids while she was gone? She could see it now, the three of them invited in for supper, the three of them drinking the same kind of drink, the three of them lying on the floor, dead! She had to get there, and fast!

"I might." Mrs. Bejweld's voice brought Amy back to reality. "Oh, yes, I remember now, my mind seems to just go sometimes. That mind of mine, eh? That," She pointed at the cabin in the pond, "Is old Mr. Yetton's cottage. Never really liked the man, Dell's brother under law or something, keeps to himself he does, at least I heard, don't see the old feller in town that often, he fishes a lot, for a living, I heard, sells what he can't use. Freezer's full o' fish, I heard. He could probably live for years on that stuff, I think. It's a trout he fishes, I heard." Amy smiled; Mrs. Bejweld would rattle off random facts for the next hour if she didn't do something. The poor old lady was more than happy to help them. She turned from the pond and looked at the older woman.

"He sounds like an interesting man, what do you say, think you can find that cabin for us?" Bejweld cocked her head, trying to remember with 'that mind of hers'. She started to pace back and forth while poking her chin.

"Lemmie think…"

Amy's smile turned into a beam. She was in good company, but was Morning?

Seth and Anne stealth walked to the house. The shadows were their friends. Their only advantage was surprise because they had the disadvantage that they couldn't use magic and their opponents could. They hid in a shadow, waited two minutes, then continued. They stuck to the blackest spots and froze when they heard a noise. Only an owl. Only a cricket. Only an engine. Wait... an engine? Someone was starting a car! If they made their getaway in it Seth and Anne would never catch up. They waited by a window. A sad, lonely voice said, "Where's Waterloo? They ignore me. How old am I, I don't seem to remember? They ignore me. My head hurts. They ignore me." The voice dropped to a whisper. "Who am I? They..." The voice started to cry, "Ignore me." Seth felt like comforting the person behind the voice. He recognized it just as Anne whispered in his ear.

"It's M." That phrase dug at his heart. He had to get his sister back, he had to. "Lift me to the window," Anne whispered softly. Seth cupped his hands to make a step for her. Her light weight made it easy for him to lift her up to the window sill. She grabbed it and swung up. Her hands worked mechanically at the window until she forced it open. "I'm going in." It felt like she was talking to air. Where was Seth?

"Be careful." His voice echoed from the shadows, but he didn't emerge. Anne slowly slid aside the curtains and slipped in. Morning's stuff cluttered the room. Her bed was made, but her door was open, just a tad. Through it she heard voices. She slid behind the door and looked through the crack made by the hinge. Bright light blinded her for a moment, but she heard clips and pieces, like: 'No, come now.' 'Never mind that, come on.' 'We have to make our escape now whether she's ready or not.' 'Sick, she can't be sick, we're leaving.' 'Evening, come on.' Anne heard Morning's voice quietly say 'Yes mother.' Mother? Evening? She must have amnesia and the old man and Dellux were taking advantage of it. Anne heard a door slam. She and Seth were too late. They were gone. She turned around to face all of M's stuff. Packing the stuff would be fun, considering the amount and the little space she had to put it in. All of a sudden, magically the items attached themselves to her. A rope on her belt, the back-pack on her back. A hat on her head, odd glasses on her ears, covering her eyes. She opened her pale blue peepers and through the glasses, she saw heat with a yellow outline. They were heat sensing glasses, but what was the scientific name? She couldn't remember. It took her two minutes to find Seth among the plants. He was lying on the ground. Anne ran to him. She took off the glasses and put them in M's pack. Seth didn't move. No! That was just what they needed, M gone and Seth hurt. She took the pack off and it hit the ground with a thud. Man! What did M have in this thing? She cautiously unzipped the big pouch and dug her hand inside. She hit something rather sharp and hard with a rubber band around it. She put the glasses back on and took it out. A bundle of CD's wrapped with an elastic band. She put them between her and Seth and dug further. Her hand once more hit something hard, a slingshot. What else was in here? A horse saddle? And a flashlight! The flashlight could help them now. She flicked the switch and shone it in the pack at the remaining items, putting the glasses with the other objects on the road. A blueberry muffin, half squished by the heavier items, M's wallet with the remaining cash from her 'emergency fund', and a fiction book. Anne took the muffin out and tore off a chunk. Boy was she ever hungry. She hadn't eaten since the apple feast yesterday at lunch, and then she'd only eaten two. She checked Seth's pulse. Thump....pa-thump... pa-thump his heartbeat pounded steadily beneath her fingertips. He must be sleeping. His breaths were long and deep. She quietly picked up the book. Why shouldn't she catch up on her history? Or math? Or science? What book was this? Anne dusted off the cover. An old picture of Greek columns was staring back at her. The Ionic column looking like someone with hypnotized eyes -- rams horns. *Ok,* she thought, *Greek history.* She quickly flipped open the cover, her fingers trembling, she read the inside cover. 'To my Morning Star, may you shine the brightest in your time of need, with love, from Dawn Starlight.' How sweet. M had a secret admirer, wait... Dawn? *The kissing-Morning-as-a-good-bye Dawn?* She thought, *cool. But why would he give her a Greek history book?* She flipped the old, thick page. It was a book of Greek myths. Interesting, she thought, and all was forgotten as she read on. The cold ground beneath her backside– forgotten. The escaping Dellux and the old man, and captured Morning– forgotten. In the stillness of the night, Anne read on. She read until she got to the back page.

"All these myths are just stories." She read aloud. "Know that God made everything in the world happen for a reason. We do not need to explain what He does; because, Him doing those things is explanation enough." *Wow,* Anne thought, *that's deep.*

Then she put the book down out of weariness. Those Greeks sure made up some funny stories to explain the world. "Oh!" She whispered, "I should wake Seth up." Then she hit her head with her hand, "Right, he's hurt, I should make him better. Hmmm..." Then she remembered the horn tip in her skin. It had helped when Seth had twisted his ankle earlier, why not now? She touched one of the bruises and felt a slight shock as her power healed him. She watched, mesmerized, as the scratches and scrapes on his battered body magically healed as soon as she touched them. He woke with a start.

"Huh?" He sounded sleepy but all better. The magic had worked. Anne quickly put all the items back in the back pack. Better leave this a secret; she didn't want people coming after her like they were after M.

"Hey!" Anne voiced her surprise. "So you finally decided to wake up, sleeping beauty. We should probably get going; they are a car ride and a night away." Seth nodded. Obviously he didn't want to talk about his encounter with the car's bumper. "Are you stiff or sore after last night?" She casually asked.

Seth got up. "No and I didn't bruise either, odd." Anne smiled; the healing magic had done its job well. Seth noticed it and knew she was hiding something. *What is that rat of a sister's friend up to?* Seth thought to himself. She was sly, who knew what secrets she hid except Morning?

Anne got up, her legs stiff, what was stopping her from using the magic on herself? She touched her knees, as if pushing them upright, and the aches were gone. She started on the trail, and then slowly turned around to ask Seth, "Are you coming? We've got bad-guys to catch."

Seth quirked an eyebrow at her, glanced at her knees, nodded, and caught up to her in three long strides. She offered him some muffin and continued to walk on the trail.

The tortoise and the hare flashed through her mind. According to the story, they'd catch up with their crooks soon enough.

Chapter X

John 14:17 _(NASB)

"The spirit of truth, whom the world cannot receive, because it does not see Him or know Him, but you know Him because He abides with you and will be in you."

I had gotten in the dark navy car late last night and, once again, fell asleep. My beaten-up body needed rest to heal properly. We weren't even out of the driveway, when we hit something. I reached for the door handle, but 'uncle Yetton' had locked the doors. I flipped the switch and pulled the door handle. The adults started yelling at me.

I got out of the car and stared at the space under it, "What did we hit? Is it hurt? Shouldn't check if it's hurt?" As usual, my questions were ignored. Mom and uncle Yetton got out and pushed me back in. "But shouldn't we check if it's alright?" I asked again.

"NO! We need to get to Waterloo as soon as possible."

"In the middle of the night?" I asked. Mom slammed the door in my face and uncle Yetton got in the drivers seat.

He looked at Mom, "Are we ready to go?"

"Yes." She growled. The car rumbled to life again and bumped along the drive. The adults in the front started talking again and I gradually fell asleep. I had fitful dreams on the car ride. I dreamt that I was the thing the car had hit. I dreamt that mom and uncle Yetton had run me right over, until I was just squish on the road. What difference did it really make? They care about that much for me, or so it seems. Was this the way it was before I fell? I remembered love, not hate.

A bucket of cold water was poured over me as a wake up call. It triggered a memory. The cold water touching my toes. I looked up to see an unfamiliar face. A man's. He was tall with ragged longish brown hair. He would have been handsome, except for the panic in his eyes, and sweat braking out on his brow. Who was he? Had he pushed me in, or was he trying to save me? I opened my eyes and was staring into an old wrinkled face. The face moved away into focus to reveal uncle Yetton.

"Wake-y, wake-y, eggs and bakey." I almost smiled at the old breakfast rhyme. Almost. I sat up. I was in another strange house, in another unfamiliar room. Would the unknown overwhelm me? I felt like a bug on the windshield, a steak in the lion's den, the first golden leaf in autumn with all the others staring wildly at me. There were three pairs of eyes on me. Uncle Yetton was one, Mom was another, and the last was a fairly old man, short and thin. Their glares dug into my heart, they hated me. But why? What had I ever done to them?

I stifled a smile, an awkward smile, and asked, "So, what's for breakfast?" My voice seemed too cheery for my surroundings. I got out of bed, my legs almost collapsing under me. They just stared, this was worse than my dream, this was torture. I died in the dream and didn't have to face the hatred and unfeeling of these people. They must've hated for a living, by the way their frowns looked permanent. But the sad thing is I couldn't imagine them any other way. I looked out the window to get my mind off their stares.

The scenery was gorgeous. Outside was a lake, a shimmering, glassy lake. Trees dotted the coastline. They were talking and splashing water at each other. This house wasn't the only one. There were many along the bank. Almost every house had a dock and a boat too! Even ours. I heard the hum of a motorboat. I peeked through the trees and saw the white and yellow blur. Those noise makers change the feeling of a peaceful lake. They bring it into action. So this was Waterloo. Water-galore, more like it. There was a water fall at the far left end, almost as big as Niagara Falls in Canada, back on Earth.

Wait, *Earth*? Where had that thought come from? Where was Earth? Was it a town, city or country?

I felt the stares of the people around me burn through my back, but I didn't care. The 'evil eye' had never worked on me. I tried opening the window. The old wood creaked as I put pressure on it. I gave it a hard push, with a grunt, and it popped free. I heard gasps and shrieks from behind me, but I climbed out the window anyway. The fresh air brought more memories back in an instant. Seth, pushing me because he lost a bet, me falling into the river; Ms. Dellux's evil eye, Mrs. Bejweld, real Mom and Dad, love, the fat and the skinny hunter after me. I surprised myself as I drank my old life's memories in. But a glance back through the window snapped me back into reality. They still thought I was an amnesiac. So, why not let them think I still was? I figured the only thing to do was pretend my memory hadn't returned, and to play their 'Evening'. I felt a cold hand on my shoulder. Turning around, I was face-to-face with the tall skinny man from the picture in the pond. Closer up, I also recognised him as the man who had come to Earth to get my 'pelt'.

I tried to keep the amazement out of my eyes, but I quickly thought of a lie to get me off the hook. "Wow, the scenery's amazing here, I can't believe I forgot it, but I must have. Was I this amazed with Waterloo as before I hit my head?" My lie worked, he thought I was recognizing the scenery, not him.

He shook his head. "You was always be'en to yous self, when yous visited twos ye-ahs back." His grammar was terrible, it was difficult to make out what he was trying to say, and what was a 'ye-ah'? A year? But at least, with my memory back, I knew what they wanted with me. They were all on this man's side; a side that ended with me dead and my skin on display in a palace. Panic returned. I looked at the lake so the man couldn't see I was afraid. I had to figure out a way to leave without it seeming too suspicious. It was an undercover job and I had to be mighty careful.

Causally I asked, "So how long have you been here?" I was thinking that I had got him good, if he really was the king's son, wouldn't he live in the castle?

"Few ye-ahs, three, four, I's is never keepin' a count a' them." Oh, well now I knew that he didn't live in the palace, but that wasn't much help.

"I'm sorry," I apologized, "I hit my head pretty hard; I seem to have forgotten your name." I turned to get a better look at his face. I rubbed my temples with my fingers, hoping I looked like I was trying to trigger a memory.

"Sully. The name's a Sully. The peeps 'round 'eez em parts cowl me Sulky but Sully'll do me just fine." Sully turned towards the house. "They's inside want chew in pronto Eve." I nodded. "Be easy on em, yous really gave em quite a scare." *Ya, right!* I thought. "Cum awn li'll Eve," He said as he pulled my arm. Sully didn't seem evil, but those were always the most likely suspects. Plus, I remembered how evil he looked that stormy night a while ago; I would never trust him. He pulled me in the house where the depression and hate and tension of the room hit me like a punch. I guess further investigation would just have to wait.

೪ა

They had trekked for hours and seemed to be getting nowhere. How far could the kids have gone? They had just gotten to the river an hour ago after packing and looking once more in the pond. Amy had picked Anne's torn piece of cloth and had walked the rough path winding by the river's edge with Nate and Mrs. Bejweld. They seemed to be passing the same poplar every ten minutes, until they got to a clearing. The clearing had no evidence of ever being used, but it still may have been very likely. The threesome stopped and decided it was time for a drink and a snack. They had stopped earlier and took some apples from the kind little tree. Each ate one and took a drink in the river, being extra careful not to fall in. Slowly Mrs. Bejweld got up.

"Oh! My muscles! My achy, achy muscles. We should get going. Things to do, people to save. I think, if I'm not mistaken, the old feller lives just in from here." She started walking in the direction she had pointed out. Amy and Nate, having no other choice, followed in close pursuit. Soon they came to the side of the cottage known as Mr. Yetton's. They snuck around. The house looked abandoned, the garage was open and missing a car. The house was torn of all noticeable human contact, except one room the threesome could only describe as Morning's room. Everything was a mess, but messy in a good, Morning-ish way. So she had been here, good. They then walked out, satisfied. They were on the path to discovery, and to M. As they were looking around the abandoned grounds, Nate noticed the tree where Anne and Seth had been hiding. He slowly walked up to it and started an investigation of his own, while the ladies were talking. He tried to climb it but only succeeded in getting more scrapes and scratches than he bargained for. Instead, he satisfied himself by looking the tree over thoroughly. He noticed some bark gone here, a little smaller than his hand. Anne had probably taken it with her when she swung off. Soon he felt eyes burning into his back. He slowly turned around, pretending to look for Amy and Bejweld.

"Man," said the tree, "What did you loose?"

"I have lost my daughter, son and a friend. I think the friend and my son may have slept in your branches last night."

"Oh," the tree exclaimed, "You mean the pretty little girl and the boy who's afraid of heights." Yup, that was Seth. "I knew they were lost!" The tree exclaimed, "They have been wandering around in circles all day chasing after a car that left last night. You humans can't tell direction very well."

Nathan smiled, "Thanks… tree."

"I'm a maple." It said.

"Well, thanks."

"I hope you find your kids soon."

Nathan gave the tree a wave, and walked away. He saw no one, not even his wife and the old woman. He was thinking over the idea to call out to them, but decided against it when he heard voices. They were not those of the two women. He slowly slid around in the trees, experimenting with shadows as he approached the voices.

"Yeah? Well we've been wandering around since sunrise and where are we? Ten feet from where we started. At this rate, we'll never find M or your parents and Mrs. B." That was the voice of a young female, if he wasn't mistaken.

A deep mans voice answered her, "And that's all *my* fault, Anne, isn't it? You led us for the first round, I led the second, lets stop arguing long enough to eat the rest of M's muffin and find the stream to get a drink." Anne? Why, that was Seth and Anne! Nate contemplated scaring the wits out of the two teens, but decided to let them know he was there by asking where Amy and Mrs. Bejweld were.

"Amy, Amy dear, where are you? Amy? Mrs. Bejweld, I'm over here, it's Nate, Nathan Star. Where could those two old women get to?" He yelled, pretending to find his wife. Soon, just as he expected, he was ambushed by two very ragged looking teenagers. They were so happy to see him. Anne was in shock. She kept rattling off random facts about what she'd heard.

"Waterloo, Ms. Dellux and Mr. Yetton, M captured, in a coma or something, amnesia maybe, so scared, never see you again, lost, car ride, Waterloo, Morning, Mr. Yetton evil, up a talking tree, hard to sleep, Morning, where are you?" Anne was devastated and needed rest and comfort. She was crying.

"Ya, it's ok, honey," Nate gently told her. He turned to Seth, "Let's go find your mother."

Seth picked up Anne and cradled her in his arms. "Ready when you are, Dad." Mr. Star walked ahead as Seth followed with Anne's arms around his neck and her head on his shoulder. Her tears were slowly soaking his shirt. He walked behind his father. *M, where are you?* He pleaded in his head and with his heart. *Wherever can you be?*

❧

That poor innocent family, torn apart by evil, it was too much for an old woman to bear. She was helping the Star family out of the goodness of her heart, or was she? Mrs. Bejweld knew not any longer. She badly wanted revenge on Ms. Dellux, for hurting her and for tearing apart the Star's. She also wanted to see her friends safe and sound.

The group had been walking for ages, it seemed. Little Anne had overheard a lot that had been said before Yetton and Dellux left with M. Mrs. Bejweld knew the way to Waterloo well, she had a cousin there. Anne had also heard Ms. Dellux's account of the cousin and, judging by the description of them, he was the skinny short man from M's peek in the pond. The group was deathly silent on the walk to Waterloo, they had no idea what they'd find when they got there. Anne's crying fits were becoming mere sobs as she strode along in the afternoon sunlight. Poor girl, Mrs. Bejweld thought, her best friend was twenty miles away in the den of the lion, and from what Anne had said, she was in a coma or had amnesia. From all Anne had recited, Mrs. Bejweld was leaning towards amnesia.

All of a sudden, Mrs. Star stopped. The rest followed and listened. They heard a noise like thunder. Seth had looked up, the sky was clear. Anne had taken her backpack off and was digging through it. Mrs. Bejweld was paying too much attention to the noise to see that Anne had taken out the horse saddle and a length of rope. She spun the rope around her hand and tried it out as a whip.

SNAP!! Everyone jumped ten feet in the air and turned around in surprise. Anne handed the saddle to a startled Mrs. Bejweld and took a step forward. She wiped a tear off her cheek, sobbed once, and snapped the rope again. The thunder slowed. Soon a mare stumbled out of the trees.

Anne took her rope and tied it around the mare's ears and head like a makeshift bridle. She put her other hand out behind her back and felt the thick, warm leather of the saddle being placed in it by a tentative Mrs. Bejweld. Expertly, she placed the saddle on the mare and tightened up the girth. Those horsemanship lessons had paid off after all. She motioned for the adults to get on.

Anne and Seth took turns guiding the mare and sleeping on the sled Amy and Nate had formed out of things they found in the forest. The journey from then on was easier on all of them. Soon Anne and Seth were both tired and the mare walked on without a guide. Anne and Seth fell asleep on the sled and the adults were snoozing in the saddle. Seth's arm was around Anne's shoulders. The day finished and night began, the horse walked on and the people slept.

Mrs. Bejweld was dreaming about ways to get back at Dellux, while Amy and Nathan were thinking about their daughter's safe return. Seth was having the same nightmare he'd had for the last two days and nights. Morning, eyes glazed over made the rock fall in mid-skip, him pushing her and her panicked reach for the railing, her limp body floating down the river. He'd dream it over and over. Sometimes he was the one floating down the river, and sometimes it was Anne. Why was he mad at Anne? Maybe because she was so perfect, maybe because she was so beautiful, maybe because he loved his sister more than her but still she was M's best friend. He knew it in his heart, though, he was jealous of Anne and her friendship with Morning.

She was dreaming, too. She dreamt that Seth hated her, that he pushed her off the bridge. She dreamt of M, and how sad and lonely she sounded through her window. She dreamt of a man with strong arms picking her up, holding her. Wait… that was real! Her eyes popped open. She was looking into clear honey eyes with brown curly bangs winding around his face. It *was* a man. He was younger than Seth; at least he looked younger, but older than Morning.

"Rats!" His low, deep, kind voice echoed in her mind. "I took all the rest inside without waking them except you." Anne smiled.

"It's okay. I can walk, you know, you can put me down." Oh! He thought, of course, he was still holding her.

She reminded him of Morning. Her hair was only a tint lighter, and she was maybe two inches taller, but the part he noticed that was not at all like M's was her eyes. This girl had pale blue eyes like glittering frost, while Morning's were a warm autumn silk. He gently put her down.

"I see Renete found you." Anne looked at him as if he were speaking gibberish. "That's my mare. She gets out and brings the lost to me quite often. What brings you this way?"

Anne debated telling the man, but blurted, "My friend Morning fell off a bridge; she's unconscious and maybe has amnesia. I need to find her. She's been taken to Waterloo, and evil people are after her." She caught herself, "Can you help?"

His blood ran cold, he felt faint, "Morning?"

Chapter XI

Matthew 5:44 _(KJV)

"But I say unto you, love your enemies, bless them that
curse you, do good to them that hate you, and pray for them
who despitefully use you, and persecute you."

"Morning, you mean Morning Star?" His voice was choked and high pitched. He was on the edge of panic. How could this have happened, she had the horn, right?

The girl looked quizzically at him. "Yeah, you know her?" She started walking towards the house. "I'm Anne, her best friend on earth." He smiled, no wonder she seemed familiar, M had talked about her so much, how could he not know her?

"M talked about you so much, I can't believe I didn't recognize you." He followed her inside, his footsteps echoing on the tile floor.

"Yep, M sure can talk, but I have no idea who you are. Have I ever met you? Morning was pretty good at keeping secrets, too." She turned to him. "Who are you?"

"Dawn."

Dawn? Was she hearing right? If she was, this was the guy who had helped M get back to Earth. This was the guy who kissed her before she left. This was her… boyfriend? "Dawn Starlight," She finally said.

He stared. How did she know? "So you've heard of me?" Anne slowly nodded, her blonde mane shaking.

"She said you kissed her."

"It was a good-bye kiss." He blurted.

"On the lips?"

"Well…" He started to blush.

"She said you held her around the waist and flew with her."

"I…" He stuttered, blushing again.

"Mistook her for your other girlfriend… um… Nora?" Anne watched as he blushed for the third time so far in the conversation. *Wow, he really must like her,* Anne thought.

"If you knew so much, how come you didn't recognize me?" He asked.

She walked to the window and looked at him over her shoulder. "Well, M and I have different views on the word 'handsome'."

"She thinks I'm handsome?" His voice went high. He loved her, and now there was hope she loved him back.

"Yep," Anne started, but he interrupted her this time.

"And you don't?"

"Well… not exactly." She admitted.

"So the man with his arms around you on the sled, is he your vision of 'handsome'?"

"Seth? Morning's brother?" She scoffed. Dawn looked at her. She gave in. "Yes, I think he's handsome, and cute, and boyish, and…"

Dawn held his hand up. "Enough," He laughed. "I have heard enough girl-talk to know that means you like him a lot."

"Oh!" Anne gasped, just thinking of something, "Was it you who gave her this book? I found it in M's backpack. It said in it that you gave it to her." She took the back pack off her shoulders and took out the book. Slowly she handed it to Dawn. His hands lovingly brushed the cover and tilted back the spine. He picked up the hard outer cover and turned it. Inside was his letter to Morning all those weeks ago. Tears filled his eyes.

"Ya, I know." Anne's voice was soft and comforting. "I miss her too." She gave him a pat on the back and Seth, in the background smiled.

She thinks I'm handsome. And cute. And boyish. He thought before turning away to wake the rest. *And Dawn thinks she really likes me.*

෴

Over the last few days I had found so much of the bad-guys plans it was scary. Sully had planned to get me through the attack on Earth. When that failed and I had come to Dovera, he sent Dellux to follow us so she and Yetton could take me. When she failed and I fell in the river, she got her brother to fish me out of the river so she wouldn't go back to Waterloo empty-handed. Their plans from there were still a mystery to me. I didn't even know how they would get me to the castle or how I would die. I missed Anne and Mom and Dad and Seth, yes even Seth. They would be frantic about me. I had to get away. Dawn lived across the water. It was called Waters there. If I could escape to there I could get back to the rest.

I have hooked up listening devices in every room. My main control centre is outside in a tree house I built yesterday and finished today. The tree loved that I'd be spending time with it but didn't really like the nails. My room has had obvious signs of rummaging. Someone is suspicious that my memory is returning, and is determined to find proof. I'm not giving them the satisfaction of getting it. I've hid all my belongings in the tree house. They'll never find them there; no adult could climb that tree, the tree wouldn't let them. I think the only reason they haven't harmed me is because they think they're brainwashing me. Even though I still answer to Eve, or Evening when they're around, I call myself Morning in my free time away from them, which is a lot of time. They treat me like a dog. They need me for show only and in between shows I can do what I wish. It takes all I have not to fall into their trap of getting me to hate. I almost hate them. Almost.

But almost is too close.

℘

"Ugh! This brainwash'in stuff takes a ton uhv time! Is she efah gunna be like us?" That was Sully. I could tell by his bad, no *horrible*, grammar. "I's is been a wondren if she's a 'membren her owld life." I felt the tension of the room. Why did they want me to be like them? They'd already said they needed my powers for evil, well, if you called a changing pelt on a wall evil. I hadn't used my powers in ages, as not to gain suspicion, but maybe they wanted me to use my powers, so they knew I still could.

"Hush up Sulk! The walls have ears, you know. Anyone could be listening." That was Ms. Dellux, and she was absolutely right. I had planted the listening devices in the walls, and I was listening in on their conversations. How did she know? My freckled face curved with my frown. Beautiful, smooth and youthful complexion, my dad had called it, along with my wide, bright joyous smile. I didn't feel joyous now. I was home-sick. I missed the love in his sky-blue eyes. I missed Anne, her freckles matched mine and her hair was honey silk. I even missed Seth and his teasing brother actions. I would trade another dunk in the river to this life any day, everyday. I missed Dawn. I hadn't seen him in ages, and I promised I would visit him next time I was in Dovera. It felt like an eternity since I had seen any of them. I had to quit feeling sorry for myself and get on with it. I had to be strong to defeat my enemies. I had to go to... sleep. How tired I was. I'd just close my eyes for ten minutes, and then I'd go inside. In... just... a... few... minutes... I'd... ZZZZzzzz. I was fast asleep.

℘

They had a list with the plans on it as not to say them aloud so no one overheard. The plans would then be destroyed. These were the plans:

- One, Bejweld and Mr. and Mrs. Star would go make a distraction in town so the bad guys would leave

77

- Two, Dawn, Seth and Anne would go to the house and retrieve Morning
- They would decide the distraction if there was anyone still at the house
- If it all came to a fight, Dawn and Seth would distract the enemy by fighting and Anne would get Morning

The plans were supposedly 'foolproof'. If anyone got left behind the plan was to go on as if nothing had happened. They were supposed to act as they didn't know each other; the two groups were separate people and events. Dawn was acting as Anne's father, while Seth was acting as her boyfriend at the retrieving scene. If they met one of Morning's captors, they were to act all 'protective' while Anne got M. If they met a lady, it would be Anne's turn for distracting, doing, as Dawn said, 'lady stuff'. Anne didn't know what to do but when the time came she figured she could come up with something. The plan was to take place at tomorrow's flea market. The troops wished each other good luck and moved to their posts. Nobody could see the two groups together, not even the night before. If the bad-guys could place the adults with the teens, they would never get M back. It was time to take action. It was time to get M back. It was time…

It was time…

I felt it in my bones. I knew it before it happened. Today was the day I'd get out. The prisoner was to be set free. I knew not how, but I knew. I packed all my things, including the ones Sully and his family had given me along with my secret sound devices and the money and jewels I had taken when they weren't watching. I had quite a bit of stuff. I gathered it all and stuffed it in the tree house. The plans were simple. Too simple. I'd get out and they wouldn't even know I was gone. I felt danger, though, animal instinct. Something wasn't quite right. I'd listened in on all their plans and there wasn't anything special happening today, except for the market. But the flea market couldn't cause any problems with my escape, could it? I heard loud voices outside. Slowly I peeked around the tree. In silhouette I saw three people. They looked vaguely familiar, yet I couldn't pin-point the names. Soon all the evil's were out asking them questions. They pointed at Sully and then the tree. All but Sully then jumped in the car. The threesome turned around and walked into the forest. I wondered who they were. I waited two minutes then swung down from the tree and stalked over to Sully.

"What's wrong?" My question penetrated thin air, he wouldn't give an answer. "Sully, I asked 'What's wrong?'" He turned around and landed a punch on the side of my jawbone.

"None a you're beetle juice, Eve." The place where he hit me burned, tempting me to fight back at him. I resisted the urge. If I gave in now, what would that bring me to do in the future? I stared at him, gaze never wavering. I knew I was getting on his nerves, but that's what I wanted. When he was stressed or angry he blurted out stuff he shouldn't. I'd heard him enough on the one-way intercom that I knew for certain he'd spill if I kept bugging and stood my ground.

"Ya, ya I've heard that before. So, what were those people here to do?" I saw his hit coming this time, and caught his wrist with surprising strength. "Sorry that side is already sore, you'll have to hit the other." Turning the other cheek, I knew I was getting at him.

"Don't you want to fight me back? You should be brainwashed by now." I put on a questioning look, hoping he'd tell farther. I let out a 'huh' as part of the act. Sully continued, just like I knew he would. "You are in no relation to me!" His bad grammar added punch to his words; they made sense in a Sully sort of way. "We was be'in a mean to you but you 'a too nice. You nev-a fell into our trap of hate. You too goody-goody!" I gaped and hung my mouth open for effect. I prodded further.

"I-I-I'm not?" I asked with a fake wavering voice and started to tear up. "But then who are you? Who am I?" I gave a shiver for effect as he replied.

"You is Morning. I is still Sully. Evening was supposed to be the evil you, but you never fell to Eve." I nodded. "Now that I've told you, you need to come an' do a job for us." Just as I thought, but I was ready for a fight, although I would only fight to defend myself.

&

The plan had worked out so far. Mrs. Bejweld made up some 'home-made wine for taste testing' to get the bad-guys to run to her. Mr. and Mrs. Star would serve them enough to keep them well away from the retrieving group. They had given the news second hand to the bad guys and they had gone running to the market. They had left one man there to look out for M. They had pointed to the tree. Anne, Seth and Dawn had walked off into the forest to get a good view of how M interacted with the stranger. Soon enough she swung out of the tree and boldly ran up to the man. She questioned the man and he ignored her. She prodded further and he hit her. It took all the two boys had to keep Anne from squealing and running to Morning's rescue. They watched on. Was this the kind of life M had been living since she had been taken? Dawn watched on in agony. He wished as much as Anne that he could go and defend M. She asked again. Was she crazy? The man made a motion to hit her again and Dawn was on his feet. This time it was Anne who held him back. He saw the punch coming, and obviously so did M. She caught the man's hand and he stumbled, sort of. He flicked his head around and started yelling at her. Poor M. She put a hand in her pocket and lowered her head. The man was confessing... something. Dawn willingly sat back down. He looked over at Seth who was intently watching his sister. Dawn looked back to Morning. Something the man said had scared her. She took a step backwards, away from the man and towards them. This time, in silent agreement, all three stood up in unison. M would have back up, but would she remember them, or fight against them? It tugged at Dawn's heart that his only love might not even remember him. They watched on, preparing themselves for whatever was to come. Morning, suddenly, turned into an eagle. All three knew from past experiences that M could defend herself when she had her powers, and that they would only get in the way, but it still hurt that they couldn't do a thing to help her. The man took a few seconds to find out what was going on, he must've thought she had lost her memory, too. He stood strong, though and started to grow. He soon was taller than the tree's.

"Sully." Dawn breathed. "The evil king's evil son." Morning turned into the largest thing she could think of, a dinosaur. She was taller than him for a few seconds, and then in one moment he was above everything. When he spoke Dawn, Anne and Seth heard his deep rumble and the words that came out of his ten foot tall mouth.

"I defeated you once, I can do it again." What? The three-some looked at each other M had never met this man. So who was he to say that he defeated her and could do it again?

"Wait, when she saw him in the pond she said he looked familiar, yet she didn't know him. He defeated her and then tweaked with her memory!" Anne guessed, shrugging.

Seth shook his head, "No, she had a fight that stormy night a couple months ago. She won. It must have been him, although I was there and I don't recognise the growing thing. He didn't do that before."

"Yeah, she followed him to Dovera last time." Dawn said. "She said he was after her pelt."

"I remember that." Seth nodded.

All three teens watched and listened for Morning's reply. "What makes you think that? I've grown stronger than you ever could have imagined and... and I know your weakness." They heard him gasp dramatically. She turned from dinosaur to dragon and hovered by his face.

"Ya right! Let's jus' zip the yappin' and cut to the figh'tin', k? Ok-ay," He pulled back his hands and brought them down hard on the ground. The ground shook, but Morning was a dragon and didn't feel the vibrations because she was in the air. She kept dodging his fists. At that moment she noticed Dawn, Seth and Anne.

She froze for a second and the man's fist came down on her. When he picked his hand up again, Morning was nowhere to be seen. She became human behind Sully's foot where he couldn't see her, but the others could.

She waved to them and yelled. "Anne, yomatchu, tata!" She spoke in their secret language so Sully wouldn't know what she said. She kept blocking his attacks as he gradually shrunk from his towering form. Anne turned to the others.

"What did she say to you, Anne?" Seth asked.

She was almost crying, "If I remember it's been five years since we've used our secret language. I'm a bit rough but I think 'yomatchu' was…yom: run, at: to, chu: open. Run to open. Run to the clearing!" Anne's voice was fast and nervous.

"What's 'tata'?" Seth questioned.

"Actually, I think it's ta, but she said it twice." Anne was thinking furiously, what was ta? "Oh. Ta was hurry. I remember she used to use it when I took so long in the public washrooms. Tata is hurry, hurry. Let's go!" Anne ran out in the clearing, surprising Sully. She gave a long female scream which made Sully look at her instead of M. Morning took her aim, and shot giant porcupine quills at him. He fell in a slow dramatic fashion. By then, Seth and Dawn had joined Anne in the clearing. Morning motioned to the speedboat tied loosely to the dock. They ran along the pier and M started the motor.

"Where'd you learn to drive a boat?" Seth asked.

"TV" She replied, then whispered to Dawn, "Can you use your ice on anyone who challenges us as I go get Mom, Dad, and Bejweld?" He nodded and Morning grunted as her brother climbed aboard and the boat tipped, "You've gained some pounds in the last how long?" He smiled, knowing his sister was teasing.

M roared the motor to life and started to speed off across the lake, the hum of the motor, thumping in sync with Dawn's heart. He had missed her so much. They all had.

Morning turned to look back at them. "I'm glad you are safe, thanks for coming to my rescue."

"Awww," Seth said, "No matter how annoying you are, you're still my sister. I had to help"

"Literally *had* to help," Anne piped up form beside him. "Your dad told him to, or else. Funny how his 'or else' works on you but mine doesn't."

"You are too pretty to carry out a threat." Seth threw back.

"Guys…" Morning warned.

"Yeah, she's pretty **and** can carry out a threat, so stop it." Dawn's deep voice sliced through the wind, "If I didn't know anything I'd say you two are in love." That shut them up. They looked at each other in bewilderment.

The boat started to bump on the waves. Then the motor made a screeching sound and bounced up, it did this twice more before cutting out. Morning tried to start it again.

"What was that?" Anne asked.

"Rocks," Dawn and Morning said at the same time.

"We bumped on rocks," Dawn clarified, smiling at Morning. He looked behind them. He saw big Sully wading through the water. "Morning, we got Sully at… um. Two o'clock."

"Huh?" She asked and came back to the stern with him.

"Sully!" She said under her breath.

Dawn looked at M and she nodded. He made an ice ball in his hands and he heard Anne gasp. "You have powers, too?" She said in bewilderment.

"Yep, now do you think I'm handsome?"

"No." Anne replied. Dawn aimed his ice ball. He leaned back and prepared to throw.

Anne whispered in his ear as he leaned past her, "But I still think Seth is cute."

His shot hit Sully right in the forehead and, like Goliath, 'one little stone went up in the air and the giant came tumbling down'… except, Sully fell down with a huge splash.

Morning turned to start the boat, but her right arm hit the wheel. She gasped in pain and held it close.

"Are you okay?" Dawn asked.

"Yeah, I just scraped my arm when I fell off the bridge." Seth hung his head.

"Hey," piped up Anne, "Let me see it." Morning slowly unravelled the bandage and she heard Anne, Seth and Dawn gasp.

"That bad?"

"Well," Dawn started.

"Yes it's that bad." Seth said. "I'm so sorry, if I'd have known this would happen, I wouldn't have pushed you."

"I wouldn't have bet you." She smiled. Anne slowly walked over, and helped M wash the wound in the lake, then she tried to heal it, but it left a nasty scar.

"Ooops. I'm still learning," She whispered.

"That's okay," Morning whispered back, "As long as it doesn't hurt anymore, I can go on. I really don't care how it looks."

"Well, I do." Anne said, wrapping it back up in the bandage.

"I'll drive, now." Dawn offered, so he walked to the engine. Seth came up and sat beside him.

"Thanks, I really don't know what I would have done without you, I have my sister back and I owe it all to you."

Dawn smiled, "That's okay, buster, it's kind of my job to take care of her." Both boys looked back at the girls and saw two women laughing together.

"I think Anne is thankful, too." Seth mumbled as the two females hugged.

Dawn tried to start the boat. Again. Again. "I don't think it's going to start." He finally said.

"It must have knocked something loose when it hit the rocks. Anybody know how to fix a boat motor?" The boys shook their heads.

"If only my healing touch worked on electronics." Anne said, then she popped to life. "Well, that's a shame, now." She said, "You boys will just have to row, I guess." She smiled.

Seth made a face, "You mean do actual *work?*" He laughed as Anne hit him.

"No, we don't have to do that, I've got an idea." Dawn said and looked hard at the lake. All of a sudden, where only water had been before, there was a tiny iceberg. It got bigger and bigger until three people could stand on it with ease. He nodded to M, "Ladies first."

Morning blushed, "A real gentleman." Then she swung her legs over the side of the boat and jumped to the iceberg. Her feet hit the surface and slid. Soon M was on her backside sliding to the edge. Anne screamed. Morning turned into a black cormorant just in time and flew up and back down to try again. Setting down carefully, she became human.

"Slippery, be careful," She said.

Anne just stared, "That was close." Then she swung her feet over the edge and lightly stepped onto the piece of floating ice. Then Dawn made another and Morning shifted her weight onto it and Seth got out of the boat. Anne got onto morning's iceberg and Dawn got onto the one Seth was on. Making one ahead of Morning, he got onto the one Anne was on as Morning got onto the one ahead of her. Soon Dawn was ahead of everyone and making more ahead of himself. Morning was behind him, helping Anne who was behind her and Seth brought up the rear.

Dawn was the first to reach the shore. Then M. Then Anne. Then Seth. Morning looked behind her brother at the string of icebergs leading to the boat way out in the middle.

"What are we going to do about the chunks of ice?" Morning asked him.

"They are normal hunks of ice, and in these temperatures they will melt before long." Dawn said.

"What about the boat?" Anne asked.

"We know that Sully can't get it. It ruins his escape…" Dawn started.

"Unless he had another car." Morning interrupted. "We don't know if the blue one was the only one they had. If it was, how did Sully get here from where he was before?"

"She's right." Anne said, "What *will* become of the boat?"

"Oh," Seth started, "Some old fisherman will come by and drag it home for parts." He laughed, joking, but Dawn said something that brought him back from his joke.

"You are absolutely right, and it will be welcome help, too. We'll know that whoever got it, it's in good hands." Then Dawn hugged Morning and Seth hugged Anne. Dawn whispered to M what Anne had whispered to him earlier on the boat about liking Seth. Morning looked at them and smiled.

Soon, Morning turned into a dragon, everybody boarded, and they flew to the marketplace to pick up the distraction group, the ice-path trailing out into the middle of the lake looked even funnier from the air.

Chapter XII

Proverbs 3:22-24 (NKJV)
"So they will be life to your soul and grace to your neck. Then you will walk safely in your way, and your foot will not stumble. When you lie down, you will not be afraid, yes you will lie down and your sleep will be sweet."

The plan had gone as, well, planned. The retrieving group had sent the evil people over, pronto. They had done their job; they had drunk the wine, encased with sleeping pills. Mrs. Bejweld's brew was famous for flavour and they had tried five before dozing off. Then the distracting group had provided beds and the evil ones had slept like logs. Then they tended to the others wanting a draft… except without the sleeping pills. Not only had they stuck to the plan, but they had made money, too! The distracting group had earned, with tips and donations, $567. Then, almost at closing time, a dragon with Seth, Anne and Dawn came to take them home. By this time the evil people had awoke; this being Yetton and Dellux. One look at the dragon and they knew Sully had lost a battle with the girl. They knew when it landed in the market that the dragon was here for the brewer and the two servers; they came to the quick conclusion that the wine was a detour, a set back, a distraction so they could retrieve the girl. Realizing this, they had Mrs. Bejweld, and Mr. and Mrs. Starr tied up and in their car in a matter of minutes. Then they drove off into the sunset. Ms. Dellux only felt a little bad about tying up her friend, but business was business, right?

❦

I had escaped, yes, but it was not over yet. We still had to get the adults in group distraction back to headquarters. I landed at the edge of the market and the four of us scattered. I was the first to find their tent. It looked closed down, but there was a note. It read:

Dear M,
We have been taken by the enemy to 'the hole' don't come too soon, they're expecting you. They told me not to leave too much evidence. You're to come all alone, no Seth, no Anne, and not even that cute kid

Dawn. Alone and unarmed, like you need weapons with your powers. You can't show this to anyone or tell anyone, so they can't come to your rescue. I'm sorry. Don't worry about Mrs. Bejweld, your father, or me. They'll keep us alive and unharmed until you come. Take your time.

Love mom.

Just as I guessed, they had seen me fly in and had taken the adults. We were still group retrieve but this time it was for them. Hopefully they'd cause a very good distraction, I might take a while. How would I tell the rest where I was going? Should I just leave? No, then they'd come after me and try to save me, they'd think I needed saving again, instead I was the saver. I stuffed the note in my pocket and gave my business to a couple of tables. I bought a muffin and a milkshake. I sat at one of the closed tables from the liquor stand. Where were the rest? We shouldn't have separated. Or they could just be looking at random tables. I waited and waited. Finally I saw Seth. Most of the stands were closed by now, what was he doing? I watched and slipped over to him without a noise. He looked nervous and maybe even scared. What had happened?

"Hey," I said walking up to him. He jumped and I was sorry I scared him. "What's wrong, come on spill." He tentatively looked around to make sure no one was watching and took me over to the side for good measure.

"They came here they hurt my Anne," *Your?* I thought. "Dawn went after her," He continued. "They hurt him. I ran, they chased me, can you help?" I nodded and, sure from his actions no one was looking, whipped into dragon.

"Hop on," I offered and he hurried on my green scaly back. "Tell all." It wasn't a 'please do' it was an order. My best friend and boyfriend's lives might be on the line.

"Ok, I was looking at some fine jewellery to get for Anne. I held up a piece and through it I looked at her. She saw me and waved. Then I saw Dawn walk over to her. He said something to her that made her mad and she stepped back, right into Sully. He turned around and bopped her on the head with his gun. He tied her up and threw her over his shoulder. He said something about needing her for later or saving her for later or something." I gave a gasp, poor Anne. Seth continued, "Dawn lunged at him and I heard the gun go off. Another one of Sully's men took Dawn and put him in the car. They put Anne on top and said something about a happy couple. I guess he thought Anne was you. Then he turned to me and pointed his gun. I rolled out of the way and ran in zigzags. I heard gunshots all around me but ran for my life. I heard them behind me but soon the gunshots stopped and I heard faint cursing. I ran and only took a breather when you came and scared me." His story made sense. But was Sully at the market when Yetton and Dellux had already taken their ransom?

"Let's go!" I flew long and hard as if I would never tire. We stopped for a bite to eat at a small gas bar in Low Valley, just on the edge of Light-fire Mountain. This wondrous natural feature was famous for its glowing stones. I didn't know where we were going or what we were looking for, but I knew that it would be easy to conceal a secret door in the mountains. Upon entering the small store, the lady at the counter yelled at us to sit where we wished. Seth chose two seats at the counter and right away ordered himself a double cheeseburger and a shake. I sat there, lost in thought, when an idea occurred to me. If the bad-guys wanted me to find 'the hole', maybe it was a place well known to the people of Dovera. When the waitress came back with Seth's meal, I took her aside.

"Excuse, me," I looked at her name tag, "Um... Bettie?"

"Yes?" She answered, "How can I help you?"

"I'm looking for a place, but I don't know where it is, could you give me directions?"

"I'll certainly try." She said, walking over. Her footsteps sounded like horse hooves on stone. Her light blonde hair flew in her face and she pushed it away. She placed her tray down and leaned over the counter to talk to me.

"I'm looking for a place called 'the hole'; do you happen to know where it is? My friends and family are being held captive there by the king's son."

She looked worried. "I don't know where the hole is. I've never heard of it. I wish I could help you. People in different parts call different places by different names, but if the king's son took your family, your best bet would be to search the castle... or at least, what's left of it."

I had never thought about that before. The castle. That seemed way too obvious, but it would make my job easier. "Thank you, can you direct me to it?"

She came out from behind the counter and I saw that she had goat legs, like a faun or satyr. She caught me looking. "I am a goat-girl, why do you look so surprised? This restaurant has been owned by my family for years. We are all half-goat."

"Oh, I didn't know. Sorry for staring, I've never seen a faun before."

She smiled and pointed out the window. "See those mountains in the distance?" I nodded, "They are the Samyon Mountains, named after our first king. He was a good, honest king." She paused, lost in thought for a second and a curl fell into her face, she brushed it away and continued. "They mark the border of the peninsula that has the castle on it. You have to pass through the mountains to get to the castle. The castle itself is carved into the face of Jagged Peak, the roughest mountain in all of Dovera. It is a hard journey for a human, but there is an easy way." She walked outside and I followed; the easier the way, the better. She pointed again. "Over there, that mountain that looks like it's glowing? That is Light-fire Mountain."

"Oh, the one with the magic stones in it that give off light?" I had heard of it from Mrs. Bejweld. It was supposed to be amazing. It was amazing.

"That's the one. It is legend that there is a secret cave that leads from it to the castle, but nobody's ever seen it. A little to the left is a road. That road will take you a little ways up the mountain and over it. Once you cross, follow it through the range and you should get to the castle in seven hours, by car." She looked around, "Or if you're walking, be prepared to spend a night." She walked back into the restaurant. I looked at the mountains for a moment longer and then followed. I was certain that the tunnel was not a legend. What better place to hide my family than a place that supposedly didn't exist. But where was the cave?

Once inside, I ordered a cup of soup and small salad. I wasn't that hungry, just thinking of my friends made my stomach flip. The waitress noticed.

"Honey, be careful. If the king has got your family, you are probably a threat to his kingdom or a rare creature that he wants for his personal zoo."

"I'm rare. I can turn into any type of animal I wish."

She tilted her head, "Even a goat-girl?" I nodded and grew goat legs. She leaned over the counter and stared. Then leaned back and tilted her head again, "Wait, *any* animal?"

I lost the legs and sat back down, slurping at my soup, "Yes, why?"

"Oh, well there's just this old legend that a creature who can be all will save us from our evil king Endrion. I always thought the name spoke for itself. End-ri-on. As in the end for all? It's sketchy, but his name is almost as scary as he is. According to the legend, you're supposed to save us. You're here to rescue us from his clutches and deliver us from his evil. He may think he's getting you for his zoo, but you are the one who will dethrone him. Oh, please say you'll help us, if only you'd see how he treats us. It's horrible." Seth glanced up from his soup, he'd obviously been listening.

"No, Morning, you can't, we have to save our family."

The girl looked so sad, glancing from Seth to me, she waved her dishrag around for emphasis, "But can't you do both? If Endrion is really holding them captive, get rid of him when you get them back. Please?" She got quieter, "We need someone to help us. Someone like you. Please?" By now everyone in the restaurant had heard.

"Yeah, help us." One man called

"Deliver us from the evil Endrion," Shouted another.

One little boy came up to me. He was a centaur, he clopped as he walked, just like the waitress. "Please?" He asked, whining just a little, "We have a mean king, he took my mama, and you are such a nice lady, can you save her. Please? Please help us?" I patted him on the head.

I smiled, "Sure, why not?" Seth gave me a glare, "Well, I can try at least, can't I?"

When it was time to leave, a crowd had gathered to wish me luck and send me off. Bettie walked up to me and whispered in my ear, "I know that the secret tunnel was supposed to be in a house, an old one up on Light-fire Mountain. And whatever you do, remember that love is stronger than any spell, stronger than any evil. Remember that, and God be with you. I'm sorry I can't go along and help you, but my place is here."

I looked at her and shook her hand, "You've helped more than you'll ever know." She bid me farewell, handing me a notebook as we left. I nodded and accepted it; it would help to organize my thoughts. I gave the girl one last smile as I walked out the door, Seth at my heels.

"What's the book for?" Seth, mumbling, asked with part of his hamburger sticking out of his lips.

"Me," I answered simply. I'd write all I did here, and all I figured out.

"We can't get rid of the king, Morning, let your common sense tell you that. He has more power than anybody here, even you. You can't do this. I won't let you."

"I can do what I wish, and why can't I try, Seth, tell me that. If I try, can't I succeed? I can help these people. They said so themselves, this world needs saving. Why can't I be their hero? Why can't I at least try?" I rushed along the road and we stopped at a bend where trees were growing in a clump. Seth laid down to sleep and I started by copying my mother's note in the book Bettie had given me when I walked far enough away from Seth that I knew he wouldn't find me. I had a blue pen in my pocket that I took out to write with. Maybe now I could share my feelings without breaking the promise not to tell Seth. The waitress was such a kind girl; I really hoped I could help the Doverians get rid of their king. Seth dozed off on the side of the road and I took the notebook out and slowly opened the cover.

Morning Star, Day 1:

Mother's note,
Dear M,

    We have been taken by the enemy to 'the hole' don't come too soon, they're expecting you. They told me not to leave too much evidence. You're to come all alone, no Seth, no Anne, and not even that cute kid

Dawn. Alone and unarmed, like you need weapons with your powers. You can't show this to anyone or tell anyone, so they can't come to your rescue. I'm sorry. Don't worry about Mrs. Bejweld, your father, or me. They'll keep us alive and unharmed until you come. Take your time.

Love mom.

Things to figure out:
- Where is 'the hole'?
- What other evidence could mom have left?
- How can I tell Seth now that Anne and Dawn are gone? I can't leave him alone, they may harm him.

Ripping up mother's note as soon as I had copied it, I looked at my notebook so far. I didn't have much to go on.

Places where 'the hole' could be:
- In a cave in the mountains
- through a secret door in a house

I remembered what Bettie had said. Those were all the possibilities I had so far. Seth started to stir. I put the notebook back in my backpack, so kindly given back to me from Anne, and bumped the saddle. The saddle! We were taking air travel when the bad guys had a car! If I was a horse Seth rode on we could take the roads, and if they had driven through the pass, we could tell by their tracks. I put my backpack on and turned into a horse. It disappeared and became part of my horsey body. Seth would never find it now. He woke and we started our journey.

∾

Where to look, where to look? I had checked off two things on my lists, and was wondering where to look next. We were stopped for a 'breather' on the side of the road. Seth had wandered into the bush to let his bladder loose and I was sneaking some write-time.

x What other evidence could mom have left? (She left pieces of her clothing and notes on the side of the road.)

x Where is 'the hole'? (From mom's notes I now know exactly, well, sort of.)

Note 1:

The 'hole' seems to be of high altitude, love mom. (The waitress said it was on the mountain)

Note 2:

They talk about mountains, love mom. (Light-fire Mountain was the closest)

Note 3:

They talk about 'the secret entrance' in a house, love mom. (Part of the 'legend' Bettie had told me)

Note 4:

I've been caught, love mom.

Note 5:

It's in Waterloo, dear, from mom.

Note 6:

Ignore note 5. It's a lie, love mom.

From what I gathered, mom says: The hole is found off a secret entrance in the mountains, in a house in the mountains, which leads to a cave in the mountains. (Which is exactly what Bettie had said) Anyway they found her out and made her write note #5 to throw me off. Mom got one more note in telling me it was a fake. Yeah, mom, way to go! I owe you. ☺

Seth slept all the way up the mountain path, but woke when the altitude started popping his ears. Following the trail was hard; I slipped often and tried hard to keep my balance. A car definitely would not have made it this far. I stumbled on a rock and we went sliding down the face of the mountain, head first, at about dusk. When we stopped we were ten feet from the only house we'd seen so far, funny how fate works that way, eh? I told Seth to stay outside and keep guard. If this was the house Bettie had mentioned, it might be guarded. Seth stepped towards me to protest but I flew in the window of the house before he could say anything. It was getting dark, now, so I used bat to find my way. I flew around in a hall and heard voices, so I slipped behind the frame of the door and eavesdropped. I heard a grunt and a screech of metal on metal. They needed to oil it, which I was guessing might be the secret door. I heard a few mumbles and then the screeching continued and there was silence. I waited one minute, two minutes, three, no sound or noise in the house for three minutes. I should be safe. I turned into mouse, the quiet, and scurried along the hall to the room. My feet made no noise as I swept the floor with my tail. I huddled beside the door for ages. My eyes covered the room, where could the secret door be? I turned around and took out my note book. In it I wrote:

House at the bottom of Light-fire Mountain, old, abandoned shack. Secret door in...

I looked in the room, how could I describe it for future reference?

...the last door on the left. It looks like an old bedroom for a queen. Where is secret door? Find out soon.

The note book was placed back in my backpack by shaky pale hands. This was it. Now, or never. I almost chose never, but thinking of the little centaur at the restaurant made me take a step in the room. I snuck around, making sure there were no traps set for me. I found a few old, rusty mouse traps, probably set by the original owner of the house, but my vivid imagination could see Sully setting them out for me when I come here as a mouse. I tapped the walls and checked under the bed. I had lit a match I had in my pocket and held it up to look around. It flickered and soon went out, I moved to the wall and lit another one. On the bedside table, I found a candle on an old candlestick. I picked it up and slowly lit the wick. The fire caught and a flickering yellow light filled the room. It was almost as bad as being in the dark, worse because the dancing flame set an eerie feeling to the room. I thought about what would happen to me if I was found in here and shivered, I had to find the others and soon, or I would lose my mind. Body tense, I checked the back of the wardrobe. It proved to be useless, no fake back or key to open anything. I checked along the edge of it, no spring to set off. It wouldn't move. I crawled under the dusty bed, but there wasn't a trapdoor or any crack in the floorboards. No ladder that dropped from the ceiling, no fake wall, no bookshelf that had a spinning mechanism. I couldn't find the door anywhere, yet I had just heard it. I did a full circle and saw something I had missed before. A closet. I reached for the doorknob, but froze, my hand still in mid-air. I had heard a creak in the floorboards and I hadn't moved. I held my breath. I felt eyes burning through the back of my shirt, someone was watching me. I slowly turned to be face to face with Sully. The yellowing teeth smiled in an evil way. His grey eyes glinted in the flickering light of the room. His dark eyebrows were darker and his hair was a curling shadow on his head. I let out a gasp of surprise. The flame flickered.

"Hello, Morning." Sully let out a sneer. "I've been expecting you." On the last word, Sully's breath blew the candle out.

Chapter XIII

Proverbs 3:5-6 (NKJV)
"Trust in the LORD with all your heart, and lean not on your own understanding; in all your ways acknowledge Him, and He shall direct your paths."

I screamed.

Sully lit another match and held it to my candle. Then his rough fingers pried mine away and he took the light over to the closet door.

"Try over here, miss." Sully's long, crooked finger pointed to the closet where I had yet to check. I slowly opened the wooden door to reveal a rusty metal door behind it. It seemed obvious, way too obvious. But, I kept my calm and wits and slowly spoke.

"You go ahead, be the leader, since you know the way." I offered him. He handed me the candle back and pushed all his weight on the door. It creaked in those same menacing notes I had heard before and swung back to reveal a dark hallway. The stones were faintly glowing. I blew out the candle and, while I was following him, wrote in my book:

Door is in closet, leads down darkly lit hall. Cold, wet stone all around. It's an almost claustrophobic walk on an ascending path. We are going deeper and higher into the mountain. The stones are glowing. We are still in Light-fire Mountain.

Silently, I slid the book and pen into my back pack. I caught up to Sully and thought if I had to be in here with Sully or alone, I'd still pick Sully. He was better than nothing, and it was so spooky in here, you could almost imagine the walls dancing to life and gaining faces and bodies. I shut my eyes tight, but the pictures were clearer on my eyelids. I opened my eyes again. A growling sounded from nearby and jumped. I winced as Sully snickered; he was enjoying the fact that I was scared out of my wits. I threw a light, teasing punch at his back, but my knuckles hit a hard, gleaming object. What was Sully wearing, was it armour? Why was Sully wearing armour? Was he going to fight? *Yes,* my brain told me, *he's going to fight you.*

93

Soon, the glowing on the walls died away and a torch was positioned every few feet. The flickering was worse than the glowing, dancing walls of the previous mountain. I crossed my arms and grew fur on my back to keep me warm, it was freezing in here.

Hours and hours later, after a long, tiring walk, the tunnel started to widen and soon it was two stories tall. I stopped for a moment to look. The room was tall and rounded. It was a glowing emerald green with intricate carvings on the wall, in the ceiling, on the floor, everywhere. Some showed dragons fighting mammoths, and others depicted scenes of love. These were carvings that I didn't understand, who did it, where did they come from, what was the reason? I saw the image of a dove repeated in many pictures. It made me remember when I had been unconscious and seen the dove in the dancing sunlight.

I felt a cold hand on my arm after a while, and again followed Sully.

"I enjoy those designs, too." A gravely voice spoke from where Sully was, he turned his face, "I could look at them for hours, but we don't have that time." *It would take more than hours to fully take in all those carvings,* I thought. "If you find pleasure in looking at that room so much, just wait, the others get better and better." Again, the emotion in his voice almost convinced me he wasn't evil, he couldn't be. But the other half of my brain kicked in and gave me a clear picture of his face this afternoon at the lake and all those feelings flew away as quickly as they had come. I walked behind Sully, wondering if my nightmares would ever end.

&

The next rooms we entered were always larger than the room before. The last one had stones glowing a pinky red. The carvings were less intricate, though they had more meaning to me. Some looked like the CN tower in Toronto, with waterfalls like the Niagara Falls in Ontario. Others looked like the Rocky Mountains, the Three Sisters, Cascade Mountain, Mount Rundle, Castle Mountain, and many more I didn't recognize. I realized that this room depicted things that had happened on Earth, things I had been a part of. I saw the Calgary tower and the Stampede. I saw West Edmonton Mall and the waterslides.

It showed a map of Canada, and the US, and had many recognizable American pictures. I could recognize the Statue of Liberty in New York, and the Grand Canyon, Lake Tahoe, the Arizona Desert, Waiamaia Canyon on the island of Kauai Hawaii, and Mt. St. Helens' eruption. Then I saw a picture of the earth from space, and then pictures from around the world. The Eifel Tower in Paris, France, was one I recognized right away. I could see the Great

Wall of China, and a building that was tilted to the side. *Probably the Leaning Tower of Pisa,* I thought. I saw pictures of Ancient Greek columns and slid my fingers over the simple Doric, the ram-horn Ionian, and the sprouting Corinthian with the fern leaves spreading out to the ocean. I could see a giant iceberg and the Titanic, hull split, sinking down into the black depths of the Atlantic Ocean. I saw Viking ships and warriors and the Romans and their ships.

All the pictures shined pink-ish red and the stone behind it glowed a dark and violently fierce ruby. It reminded me at once of war and heat and blood-shed. I felt uncomfortable with the room, not knowing how to feel. I was proud that Dovera had a whole room dedicated to Earth and our amazing accomplishments there, but I was sad that they didn't show the love of everyday life. How much we cared for each other made up all our daily lives, if they didn't get that, they didn't know Earth at all. Disappointed, that's how I felt. I looked on, and saw the moon and the sun. I saw man in space in those big, bulky spacesuits. I saw the Canada-arm and a rocket and the tremendous amount of smoke and flame used just to get that thing into orbit. I saw the Apollo # whatever and all the planets behind it. Was it Apollo 13, 11, or 12? I was too young to remember those facts, and for that I was sorry, it would have been nice to know all of Earth's history, like it was here.

I saw a sunset and three wooden crosses on a hill. This sight brought tears to my eyes. I looked on and saw a close-up of the two thieves on either side of Jesus and Him crying up to the heavens for our forgiveness. Man hadn't changed after the Son of God came; they still stole goods, committed murder and adultery, and turned away from the one true God to false gods. I reached out and brushed Jesus' face. I wasn't brushing the face of God, I was brushing cold stone. Again, Dovera didn't get the love on Earth at all. They only saw the facts; the empty, raw facts.

I turned to Sully. "Next room please," I said through the lump in my throat. I disliked him more than ever now. And it was dislike, not hate. I would love my enemies as myself but that didn't mean I had to like them. He knew Earth not. He knew love not, but he would know soon. I would show him, soon. I would counteract hate with love. I would get those I loved back. I would!

૭૭

He hardly saw the rooms as he passed through them. His mind was on the girl. She was possibly being led by him to her death, and yet she took time to look carefully at every wall, every room, and every design with heart, with feeling. He couldn't understand it. She was supposed to hit him, pound him with her anger, but she was calm and loving, sweet and kind. She was the compete foil to his temper and hate; she was the opposite of his anger and frustration. It angered even him more to see her like that. He felt like hitting her again, but even that hadn't closed the gap. Something was missing from his life, something she had and he didn't. Maybe he should turn back now and spare her life, wait why was he thinking those thoughts? He hated her, did he not? Maybe her love and kindness was wearing off on him more than he knew.

He heard her slow, quiet quiver of a voice and was brought back to reality. "Next room please," was her quiet plead. Tears were flowing down her cheeks. Something had upset her. He looked around, wondering what. His eyes were met with pictures of a foreign land. Earth. Was that Morning's homeland, was she homesick?

Why should he care, common sense pushed in, why? He knew not, but he did, he did care for the rare beauty standing in front of him, and that scared him more than any enemy.

Chapter IVX

Psalms 34:4 <small>(NKJV)</small>

"I sought the LORD, and He heard me, and delivered me from all my fears."

I took out my note book and wrote,

> Caves after hallway, they show drawings of different realms and worlds. Earth is there, but the carver didn't know love. Earth has a red-ish, pink-ish glow to symbolize hate or blood-shed (I don't know which), while the caves before each glowed a different colour. I dislike Sully more. His evil must be wearing off on me. I must be strong; I'll fight the urge to be like them. I'll be myself, I'll stick up for who I am.

I read over what I'd written so far. 'Places where 'the hole' could be', I could scratch and check that column, now. I did,

> Places where 'the hole' could be:
> √ In a cave in the Mountains
> √ through a secret door in a house

I underlined them for extra emphasis. My pen started to run out of ink, I shook it, but it was gone. I dug deeper in my pack for another pen. I took out a handful; Black… red… purple… green. No blue ink. Oh well, I'd use purple. That was an interesting color. Sully turned to look at me. I was holding the purple pen up; thank goodness my notebook was in my pack.

"Um…" I racked my mind for possibilities why I would be holding up a purple pen in a cave. "Um…I want to write my name on the wall." I knew it sounded dumb, and stupid, but if I had paused too long, he'd wonder.

"You can do all in your power to try, but pen often doesn't show up on rock." He stepped closer to search it, "…Especially purple." I nodded; he'd bought it, good. I put the pen to a blank space in the wall and scratched it on the rough surface… again… Nothing happened. No ink came out.

"I guess you're right." I gave him a nod and placed the pen back in my backpack.

"You know, I'm going to have to search that thing, sooner or later." He said, pointing to my backpack.

I pulled it closer to me. "No."

"Oh yes I am, and I might as well search you, too. You weren't supposed to bring weapons."

I all of a sudden noticed his grammar was fine again. "Your grammar seems to have improved quite a bit and you know if I'd have brought any weapons, wouldn't you think I'd have used them by now? I've had plenty of opportunity." I snarled back at him. He stepped closer, and closer, until we were nose to nose. His hands, in one quick motion, had placed themselves firmly on my shoulders. I struggled to free myself from his grasp. Once I stopped struggling, one of Sully's hands moved from my shoulder and touched my side. I flinched, waiting for my chance. His touch was scary, even though his hands were usually cold; they seemed to freeze every part he touched. His lips parted and started to close down over mine. He was going to kiss me? Not on my watch! I saw his eyes close and then I kicked him, I don't know where, but it did the trick. He let go of me and grabbed whatever part I'd pierced with my sneaker. A soccer kick, usually not accurate but very powerful, had saved me: the toe-hack. I took no time in freeing myself from his flailing arms and ran in the opposite direction we'd come from, which hopefully led to my family and friends. I ran until I came to a larger room than all the ones before it. Its walls glowed red with hate and fear. It looked like the stalactites, or were they stalagmites, were reaching out to grab me. This room was taller than the last ones, and it had fire dancing along the walls. I looked up and could see a balcony for the second floor. This room was bare of drawings and furniture. I felt as if I was the only one in here. I guess I could describe it as a ballroom, tall and spacious, with a balcony for the band or the host, but fiery red. Even the floors were the dancing red, and I could feel the heat. But it wasn't like Mrs. Bejweld's 'Dovera' fire that didn't burn to the touch, this was Earth fire that caused destruction and wreaked havoc.

A flash of silver shot through the room, I thought someone was shooting at me, but the silver parted to reveal my family and friends on the dance floor. Mom and Dad were in each others arms, dancing a slow dance. Anne and Mrs. Bejweld were doing the bunny-hop behind Dawn. Seth... Seth? Seth was there, jigging and jiving to his own made-up beat. I thought I had left him outside... They looked so happy, could Anne have been knocked out and Dawn shot?

"Join them." The booming offer came from all around me, seeming everywhere and nowhere, all at the same time. I used my animal instinct to trace it; it came from the balcony. I didn't turn my head, but fixed my eyes on the dancers instead. Slowly I grew eyes on the back of my head, who was my challenger? I saw a tall man with a fire engine red cloak on. Typical, I thought, considering his taste in room coloring. His beard was a silvery grey, which glimmered in the bright room. His eyes, the typical heated red of his surroundings, stung me. He was fat and out of shape. It was as if he was the walls and had just slid out of hiding to bug me. He could be described as looking like a wizard of some sort. A golden band was sitting on the top of his head and spikes were protruding from his hair, how awful could he be that he couldn't even wear a crown right? Could this possibly be the *king?* If he was, I knew what he was up to. Get me to dance with my family and then I'm stuck with him for eternity and nobody gets saved. *And I get pinned to the wall,* I thought sourly, *well not today!* I stomped my foot. *Not how it's going to happen, old man!* I focused back on the dancers, the extra eyes receding.

"No" My simple reply must have pushed him off balance, for he took a while to respond.

"Hmmm… you are strong." The voice echoed the deep thought; if he was trying to tempt me, but my answer would always be 'no way'! The silver flashed through the room again, and this time I was ready, I didn't flinch. I stood my ground. The dancers turned into partiers. Mom and Dad were sitting at a table with draft glasses in their hands, sipping and talking. "How about now?" Anne and Seth were kissing, *eww!* Bejweld was holding a microphone and singing. Dawn looked right at me.

"No" I stuck with my answer. Dawn's mouth moved, he leaned toward my rigid, still form.

"Join us, we're happy." He pleaded. This guy knew how to get at me.

"No" I forced it out. I had to, if I didn't respond he may have taken it as a 'yes', I may have taken it as 'yes'. I heard the old man growl, I was on his list, I knew it, but all our lives depended on me and how I acted in these last few minutes. *Lord,* I prayed, *give me the courage and strength to do what is right here, help me save my family, friends and all of Dovera from this nasty king who abuses his power over the country.*

"Now?" He boomed as the room faded and brightened again, showing my family doing forced labour. Mom was drying dishes as Mrs. Bejweld washed them, continually, while Dad was sweeping up the glass as mom dropped them into unloadable cabinets. Anne was tiring, I could tell, from dodging around the glass dad flung at her from the dustpan, over and over. Dawn and Seth were carrying heavy furniture up and up continually winding carpeted steps. They struggled and almost fell down, but held their balance and continued up the steps. As soon as they took a step, they were back where they started, it was like an escalator of doom.

I screamed and ran to the steps to help them. I put my arm around Dawn and he snarled at me I pulled back and ran over to Seth. He dropped his end of the couch on my toe and looked satisfied. I started to cry, why did they hate me? I raced over to the others and took the broom from Dad, pulling it to stop. Dad yelled at me. "It was almost clean. I could have done it without you!" He slapped my face and I handed the broom to him once more. My face burned.

The room faded and brightened again, like lightning. Now they were all fighting. Seth hit Dad, who backed up and stepped on Mom's toe. She hopped around and bumped Dawn who spun around and punched Dad. The lights blinked. On, off, on, off, on, off. Each time they blinked on, somebody I loved hit another somebody I loved. It was horrible.

"STOP!" I screamed at the top of my lungs. My throat hurt. Everybody froze as the word ricocheted off the walls in an echo until it faded out. The fires on the walls grew in intensity and the heat took away my strength. "Stop." I whispered as the flames sputtered up, clawing at the walls, climbing higher, they licked the surface and all the lights went out. The only illumination was the wicked fire casting an orange, flickering glow on the place that left it in gloomy despair.

Evil laughing erupted from the balcony above.

"What do you want me to do?" I asked the man in a quiet whisper, falling to my knees. He was way more powerful than I was... wait... power; the energy stick that Sully had back home. If only I could have it, I might have enough strength to beat him, but I had no idea where it was, and if I did, I would probably never get to it in time.

"Ha! You fail." The sharp words cut through my concentration. "You don't have to do anything for me but you have to die to save them." He pointed with an ugly crooked finger at the people around me. I held my head down.

"Why." I asked. It was quick, sharp and it bounced off the hating walls like a ball on a ping pong table, except the echo gained intensity until the walls were screaming and mocking me, 'why?' 'Why?' 'Why?' 'WHY?' The fire burned brighter and hotter. And brighter and hotter.

"Why?" I whispered. The echoes slowly faded out.

"...Because you are a threat to my empire, why else? You came in and ruined the world. You have broken my laws."

"I follow God's laws." I yelled with a last ounce of energy.

"Arrrruggghhh!" He yelled. The king of Dovera obviously wasn't a patient man, so if I could wait him out, I'd be safe. I remembered what Bettie had told me at the restaurant earlier: Love is stronger than any spell. If I loved them, I would have to do this.

"Oh, you do, do you. Where has He gotten you now, huh?" The 'huh' made me think he was American, which made me think of home, which made me home-sick, which almost made me cry.

"Eh?" I answered quietly. I knew I was getting on his nerves; he reminded me of Sully in so many bad ways. I just hoped he couldn't keep his temper any better than his son, or I was in trouble. I was running out of energy, and fast.

"Bring in the arrow." He ordered someone behind me. I held up a quivering hand.

"How am I to die, oh dumb-crack king of Dovera?" It made him madder. He couldn't wait to pulverize this little creep, then he could destroy the rest and it would be over with. Sully hobbled in with a bright red arrow.

The workers had stopped work to watch. They pierced me with their accusing looks. I hoped, at the end of this they would know I loved them.

"You see this arrow?" I got up and turned to look him in the eye. The heat of the room was making me sweat, but the 'king' of Dovera seemed to be quite at home. *His heart must be made of stone, because if it was ice, it would have melted already,* I thought. That made me smile. I just had to tell myself jokes to keep my strength up.

"Yes, I see your stupid arrow." I answered, giggling on the inside.

"This is no ordinary arrow," He hissed

"Which is why you're using it on no ordinary girl?"

"Quit talking back!" He bellowed.

"You sound like my father, except he was trying to teach me because he loves me." *Plus, I am good at talking back.* I thought, *at school they called this form of argument 'debate'.* The word 'love' echoed around the room and the man screamed in agony. Sully ran in again and put a gag over my mouth. *So even speaking the word has an effect,* I thought.

"Now, where was I? Oh yes; no ordinary arrow. Once embedded in your flesh, my arrow will burn your insides out and only your pelt will remain. And I will put it in my castle to hang on my wall forever." I wriggled out of Sully's grasp and ripped off my gag. He ran away from me.

"I see. A *fire* arrow, very *original*, don't you think, considering the house you live in."

"Oh, will someone shut her up?" The 'king' roared.

"For good, daddy," Sully appeared out of nowhere, yet again and hit me on the face. My cheek burned, but no more than it had last time. "Do I shut her up for good?"

"NO! That is my job. Bring me my bow. I will shoot her now."

"May I say good-bye, first?" I asked nodding towards the frowning crowd. The king nodded and I slowly ambled over to them, tears in my eyes. I gave Seth's arm a quick squeeze and gave him a long hug. "I love you more than you know, older brother. I've looked up to you for so much. You were my role model for all those tomboy years. I love you." I gave one last squeeze and let

101

go. I moved towards Mrs. Bejweld. "Thank you for everything and all your help in this, I'm sorry I got you into this." I gave her a quick hug and she flinched under my grasp. She finally couldn't stand it and pulled away, leaving sadness in a wave to wash over me. I squeezed Mom and Dad in one bear hug of love. They pushed me away and the tears flowed freely from my hazel eyes. "I love you, too." I whispered. Anne took a step back as I approached her. I held my hand out and she shook it tentatively. The smile I gave her was only met with more frowns. Toddling I walked to Dawn. I gave him a kiss on the cheek and he wiped it off. "I love you, too." I brushed his cheek with my hand.

Turning around I saw Sully. He sneered in my direction; I just smiled through the tears. The bow was carried up to the king who already held the fire arrow. My life was to go, now, as fast as the sunset. Amazing for a moment, and then its gone, and all that's left is darkness and cold. Halfway up the steps I turned around and blew one last kiss at my family and friends; I made it look like I was really going to die, when I'd rather fight to the death. I had found the way to stop them. A hand rested on my shoulder and steered me back on the ascending walk. I knew all the things in my backpack as well as the calluses on my hands, and I was ready to use them.

"Wow, that's dedication..." I heard the king of Dovera say. "She is loyal to them even when her life is on the line. You could learn a thing or two about loyalty from this fine lass, me boy."

"It's love, not loyalty, ugly king of Dumb-era" I would bug the stupid king forever. "You don't know about that do you?" I was at the top of the staircase, now, and I spun to look back down at my family. "Love the Lord your God, the King over all kings, and you shall be saved." I spat it out and turned to the king. He was taller than me, but I didn't care. "Even as you are above me now, the Lord your God is above you always in heaven." He turned and pinched his son, Sully.

"I thought I was the highest in reign of Dovera. No one being is above me." He stepped closer to me, laughing.

"I love the Lord because He has first loved me. He loves you and cares about your out come even if you care not for Him." I replied. Every time I said the word 'love' it echoed and the fires on the walls stopped flickering and slowly died.

"He *loves* you, does He?" The king flicked his wrist and the fight was on. I used my animal instincts to determine when Sully handed him the bow and how long it would take to string the arrow. It almost hit me, but the dove I had seen so many times appeared out of nowhere and caught the arrow in it's talons. It flew away towards the wall and disappeared, and along with it, the fire arrow. The king gasped and stared at me.

"Yargghhh!" He screamed and hurled a fiery orange ball in my direction that I dodged and flew around. It crashed into the fiery wall.

I turned to the two stunned men. "Where is the rest of the gang?" I questioned as he brushed his hand and ten more Sully's appeared.

"The rest were killed for being inconsiderate." *Aww*, I thought, well at least I wouldn't have to deal with Yetton and Dellux, although breaking the news to Mrs. Bejweld would be hard.

The Sully's all started to grow at the same time... I knew how to defeat them already from past experiences. I flung spiky balls of porcupine quills at them and, one by one, they crashed into tiny pieces, except for the one true Sully, who was plucking the thorns out of his arms.

"...Too easy, come on, give me what you've got. I know Sully isn't your best weapon." I said, landing in an open patch. I dug through my backpack. I found the CD's in the elastic band. Standing, I dodged the many clay birds with fiery beaks that were thrown at me. Then I cut the elastic with a claw and flung one like a Frisbee at Sully. It worked by getting him to jump out of the way.

"Well sadly, when he didn't come back with you, I punished him. He hasn't quite been on the ball since." Boy, this king did a lot of killing and torturing and punishing. I'd hate to have him as a father... or a king. Now I knew how the people of Dovera felt. "Let's see how you do against your own kind." With another silver blast my family and friends were clad in armour and ready for battle. "Don't you need armour?" He asked cautiously.

"No!" I spat. "I've got God on my side, with Him, anything is possible. I've got His armour on, you lug-head; have you ever read the bible?" I spun a CD at him and he caught it.

"Not good enough for me... Attack!!" He ordered the gang to attack me. Crushing the silver disc in his hand, he gave an evil smile. I couldn't fight my own family! It wasn't civilized. Dodging all their attacks at once took all my power. I flew up to the ceiling and clung like a bat to the stalactites. Once attached to one with my claws, I pulled and it jerked free. It fell and caused more to fall, encaging my family in a rugged circle. They started clawing at it to get to me. I remembered that they were under a spell that could be broken with love.

I sang a song that I remembered from all those years ago when I was in Awana. First I sang it quietly to myself, then louder so the 'king' could hear.

"Love the Lord your God
With all your heart and all your soul and all your mind and
Love all of mankind as you would love yourselves
And love the Lord your God

With all your heart and all your soul and mind
And love all mankind
We've got Christian lives to live
We've got Jesus love to give
We've got nothing to hide
Because in him we all abide." It was one of my favourite songs of all time. I listened as all the loves echoed off the walls, but the fire was slowly returning. I thought of the set of verses in the Bible that said 'love' the most times. Would that stop the fires and break the spell?

"First Corinthians 13:4-8: 'Love suffers long and is kind. Love does not envy. Love does not parade itself around puffed up for all it's done. Love does not behave rudely. Love does not seek its own. Love is not provoked." Then, another voice joined me, "Love thinks no evil." And another voice joined, "Love does not rejoice in iniquity, but rejoices in the truth." And another, "Love bears all things," And another, "Love believes all things. Love hopes all things. Love endures all things. Love never fails!'" I whispered fiercely, "And neither will I." I stood and faced the king and raised my head to look him in the eyes, I turned and winked at Dawn.

"Let's do this." He whispered. I flung the rest of the CD's at the king and grabbed the slingshot. I heard a voice yell out behind me. I would know it anywhere. It was my dad's.

"'Verse thirteen," He said, "'And now abide by Faith, Hope and Love, these three; but the greatest of these is Love'." The last 'love' echoed around the entire structure. Dawn threw ice balls at walls and snow and rain at the fires. And, at last, the last of the flaming walls fell down. It cooled the room and the heat and smoke subsided to reveal a palace instead of a cavern. The stalactites were traded for statue angels and the balcony for a throne. The mountain vanished and the castle shone with wonder.

"What do Star's do best?" I turned around and shouted.

My family smiled. "Shine!" They screamed in unison. "Shine God's light in the darkness."

I saw the king. He was trying to sneak out, but his cloak was caught on a rock. I picked up the slingshot and a piece of rock and shot it. It bonked him on the forehead. "I hope that knocked some sense into him, but if it didn't, I'm taking him and Sully to the dungeon... Speaking of which, where *is* Sully?" I looked around the room. Noticing a pen-shaped object, I recognised it at once as the energy-giving thing I had found a few months before. So Sully had been the man sent to kill me. I knew it! I ran over and picked it up. Hearing a scream, I tightened my grip on it.

"Graaah!" Sully screamed again as he ran out of his hiding place and tackled me. I slithered into a snake with the pen in my jaws and then flew as a hawk to the ceiling, pen in my talons. Sully grew and I dodged his fists as he grabbed at the pen.

"Give me back my energy-drainer, you nincompoop!" Oh, so he could make it drain energy as well as give it... that made me think: If he could do it, why couldn't I? I set down and turned into my human form.

"If you want it so much, why don't you come and get it." I held it up and waved it around. "And nincompoop yourself, *Sulky*!" He growled and shrunk to my size. I pushed the button. This was just like the dream I had when I first came to Dovera, Sully and me fighting over the energy-whatever-it-does stick. I held it away from him and he grabbed at it. I was still taller than him, but he was still heavier. He sat on me and I turned into an elephant so it didn't hurt. He slid off onto his behind and whimpered.

"Awww, poor little Sully, he can't get his glow-stick back from a *girl*!" I teased, turning back into me. He jumped up and grabbed Anne. She gave a shriek. Seth lunged at Sully and all chaos broke loose. Sully threw Anne at me and hit Seth. Anne fell on her hip beside me and screamed.

The men: Dad, Dawn, and Seth, were now in an all-out fight with Sully and the boys on my side kept hitting each other instead of Sully. *This is almost as bad as a few minutes ago,* I thought. He shrunk and grew and punched when someone came close, and then shrank and grew again, avoiding all hits and kicks and making the men bump into each other. Dawn threw an iceball and accidentally froze Dad's arm. Anne and Mom, and good old Mrs. Bejweld were screaming their heads off at the boys, trying to encourage them to actually hit Sully, not each other. I just stood there. I had the energy stick and Sully tried to grab it, but Seth pulled him back.

I stood absolutely still, anger brewing until I started to blink. Seth, having seen it before, wasn't as petrified as the others. This time, though, I was so mad that my blinking made a sound, a roaring, growling sound. I screamed and the noise echoed off the walls. I blinked for a total of ten seconds, using up every horrid, fierce creature I knew, and by then everybody had froze in mid-step (and in some cases mid-hit) and everybody was silent. Everybody was staring. Sully broke from the amazement first and weaved his way through the others until he was in front of me. I had him right where I wanted him.

His hand reached out and everyone held their breath. "Give me the energy stick," He pleaded, "So I can renew my father's empire." His hand wavered in mid-air, waiting for my response.

I fingered the orange glowing stick, and bringing it behind me I saw his eyes widen, he actually thought I was going to give it to him! I twirled it like a baton and then calmly answered, "No." I used my forward momentum and jabbed it into his stomach.

"You don't know the power of my energy-transfer stick! You don't know..." He cried out before he fell over. He looked up at me. All his energy was gone. His head fell back onto the cold, hard stone.

I walked over to a staircase going down and read the sign on the wall, "And oh, look at that, Sully," I said, turning back to the others, "The dungeon here has a power-draining feature, too, so you can't grow and break out on us." Everyone laughed. I pointed to Dad and Dawn. "Will you two help me clean up this mess?" They nodded and we took the two men down to lock them in the dungeon.

ری

Anne, meanwhile, touched Seth's wounds and healed him and told him of her powers and how she had gotten them. He was amazed and asked if it was her who had healed him after he was hit by the car. She nodded her head and blushed.

"I thought an angel had come down from heaven to heal my wounds. When I woke up and you fixed your sore muscles with a touch, I kind of guessed... Thanks." Anne blushed at Seth's words.

"You're welcome, Seth. You were very heroic back there. When Sully had me, you rushed up, not caring what could happen to you. You were very brave." She put her hand on his chest. Now it was his turn to blush. The two older women behind them were whispering and gossiping already. Seth put his arm around her waist and led her out onto the balcony.

ری

As soon as I got to the bottom of the stairs, I knew that something was wrong, I could feel it. Rounding the corner, I looked into the first jail cell and saw three Minotaurs. I gasped and ran to the next one. It contained five fauns. The next one contained talking bears and wolves and foxes and leopards and tigers and dogs. Another had Unicorns and Pegasi. Another had dragons and yet another had griffins. Others were full of bugs and birds and one at the far end held centaurs. I looked closely and saw a female, probably the little centaur's mommy. All these creatures were crammed into the small confinements of jail cells! So this was king Endrion's zoo. I gasped and all the creatures started to stir.

"Who's there?" One Minotaur strained to ask, "Let me be, leave us alone." The talking beasts started to wake and they growled when they saw the king.

"What are you doing with him?" A faun asked, peeking out between the bars.

106

"I'm giving him your cell." I answered. "How do the doors open?"

A dwarf glared at me, "They don't."

The dove flew in and dropped the fiery arrow at my feet. I gently picked it up and touched it to the bar on a one of the cells. The metal melted away to a sizzling gloop on the floor.

"Does that work?" I saw the hope in the dwarf's eyes.

"I'm making sure it will work, you guys look like you want out." I melted all the cages and soon I had almost a hundred animals and beasts gathered around me watching as I put first Sully, then the king in an unused cell. Then I put manacles on their hands and feet and slammed the door shut. A cheer rose up from the creatures. The centaurs offered to give me a ride up, but I declined.

A griffin stalked up to me and hissed, "Thanksssssss for ssssssaving Dovera. I am exxxxxxtremely grateful to you for resssssssssscuing usssssssss."

I smiled at it. "You are welcome, now go, run, fly, you are free, you no longer have to stay in the castle, enjoy the world. Go." The creatures rushed up the stairs and around the corner and were gone.

The centaurs galloped at the front with the Unicorns and Pegasus' trotted along behind, and the talking animals and Minotaurs were racing up the stairs closely behind. The griffins followed the dragons and the dwarves walked out last. They were people and had manners. They calmly strode up the steps and into a world they thought had forsaken them.

Dad stared in amazement at the fairytale creatures that were really real. He slowly walked up the stairs behind them and Dawn followed, smiling to himself that the world he knew was safe at last.

I stayed and looked at the sad dungeon once more. "Take care of your prisoners, dungeon." I patted the wall gently, "You never know what might happen." I walked up the stairs and out into the light. Walking to the balcony, I looked out on the kingdom. Griffins were flying in the air, centaurs were rearing up and fauns were bowing down. All manner of talking creatures thanked me for freeing them from the evil king Endrion. People were gathering and cheering. I looked closely and saw the little centaur clinging tight to his mother's leg. All was well. The world was back to the way it should be.

Chapter DX

John 8:32 (NKJV)

"...And you shall know the truth, and the truth shall set you free."

When I returned to where the others were waiting for me, Anne was holding the funny hat with the pocket in it. Everyone was gathered around and looking at something. I walked over and she handed it to me.

"I found this in the hat. It's addressed to you."

I took the paper from her and slowly unfolded it. It was a thin, delicate paper, with intricate designs and beautiful colours. It read, "Morning, My child, you have done well. You have shined My light even in the deepest darkness. And I say 'It is good.'" After finishing the note, I read it again in my head. "Wow."

"Yeah," said Anne, "Seth and I were walking out on the balcony here and a light blinded us. Soon a dove flew down the column of light and in its beak were branches, olive branches, and in it's talons was your hat. It placed it on the rail and flew back up the pillar of light. When it was gone, your hat was still sitting here. I think it's a message from God."

"Dove?" Mrs. Bejweld spoke up, "Did you just say a dove?"

"Yes," Said Anne, "I did."

Mrs. Bejweld turned to me, excitement written on her face, "Don't you see?" Everyone in the party shook their heads except Dawn. "It's a miracle!"

"A dove!" Dawn exclaimed, "A dove created our land. A dove always comes to save us, always helping, never taking any credit for any of it's deeds. No one has ever talked to it, it never talks to anybody. It is our Silent Savior. Many think it is God."

I nodded. "I can't believe it."

"Hey! Look." Anne said. I looked over the edge of the balcony and saw hundreds of people gathering, and not just people, but magical, fairytale creatures, too. The creatures I had saved had proclaimed the freedom to even the farthest reaches of the world and were now gathering with the people to see us. "They are here to thank you for defeating the evil king. Through you, God preformed a miracle that these people have been praying years and years for." I smiled.

"I did something good that helped everyone." I watched the griffin's fly circles and loops in the air, thankful for the chance to use their wings.

"Yes you did." The deep voice behind me was startling.

I spun around. "Dawn? Oh, I just forgot, Seth said you were shot at the marketplace. Are you okay?" He pulled up his sleeve to his shoulder and I saw a round scar. I gasped. Then he held out something to me in his hand. I took it and felt a cold round ball. It was the bullet. I closed my hand and looked up at him.

"Yes, I'm fine, thanks to your friend, here." He nodded at Anne.

"Well, you took a bullet for me, there had to be something I could do to repay you. After all, it was your unicorn horn that gave me the power in the first place."

"Thanks." Dawn turned back to Morning. "Even though we were under that king's spell, we were still aware of what was going on. You were amazing and all those things I had to say, and all those things I had to do, it wasn't me."

"Yeah," Dad agreed, "You were amazing, pumpkin."

"You certainly were." Mrs. Bejweld said. "Um… can I ask the plants to grow here again, just to make it more beautiful?"

"Go ahead," I said, "It's all yours." The vines smiled at me and spread out over the stone walls, hugging the castle again, welcoming it back to the happiness everyone else was enjoying.

I turned to Dawn again. "I love you."

He put his hands on my shoulders. "I love you, too. I have loved you ever since I picked you up by mistake. And you know…" He combed a hand through his curly dark hair. "I knew all along it wasn't Nora; you are a lot lighter than she is, and a lot prettier." He held me close and bopped me on the nose. I smiled and looked into his eyes. I hugged him tight. He leaned his head down and his curly hair covered our faces. He kissed me, and it was just as sweet and breath-taking as the last one.

Seth cleared his throat and I snapped my attention back to the family standing on the balcony. "Get a room." He teased and then asked, "Who shall be king now?"

"You," I giggled. He just stared. "The new king was to be the first one of us that asked, proving to be the one who thinks about and cares about Dovera. You asked, therefore you're king." I ran to the balcony overlooking Dovera and yelled to the people and creatures below, "All hail your new king! Long live King Seth!" Echoes rained about the land. 'Long live King Seth!' 'Long live King Seth!' 'Long live King Seth!' He took his arm off of Anne and went over to look. Everyone was cheering his name.

"See?" I laughed. He turned and looked at me. Then he nodded. "All you need now is a queen." I glanced at Anne, who blushed, and took a step back. Even before Seth spoke, I knew who he was going to pick.

Seth gaped. Anne smiled and blushed some more. "Me? King?" He still couldn't get his head around it. "Me? I haven't even finished College yet and *I'm* to be a *king?*"

"Yes, *you!*" I said with emphasis, laughing and gave him a push towards Anne, "Now get a move on!"

He walked over to Anne and got down on one knee, still looking bewildered. He took her hand in his and asked, "Anne Walters, will you come and live in Dovera, sacrificing everything to be my queen?"

She giggled. "I thought you'd never ask. I will, as long as I can bring mother and father."

Seth smiled, "That can be arranged." Then he stood up and kissed her and I averted my gaze to the crowds of people and creatures still gathering around the castle gates.

I grabbed the old king's crown from the rubble, dusted it off and placed it on Seth's head. Mrs. Bejweld went to the throne room and brought back the queen's crown and placed it on Anne's head. Then she stepped back and bowed her head in respect.

The new couple moved to the front of the balcony and I yelled, "Long live King Seth! Long live Queen Anne!" The crowd screamed and cheered and threw up their hats. It was a gorgeous sight. I smiled and ran into Dawn's arms. He swung me around and around until I was dizzy. He put me down and kissed me again.

"I thought I'd never find a love like yours, but the old man's prophesy came true. I know what true love means and, along the way I've found true love. All thanks to you. I found hope, faith and love, but the greatest of these is love." The happy word echoed around the castle and it didn't seem to be mocking us anymore.

I smiled at him. "I found my true love, too."

Dawn looked over the land below us. "It's over, my little angel, it's all over." And in his arms looking out over a happy Dovera I could truly believe that. I hugged him tight as if I would never let him go. He hugged back and kissed my head.

"I love you, Dawn Starlight."

"I love you, too, my Morning Star."

♥

Back in the dungeon, two unhappy men were chained to the wall, side by side.

"What is all the cheering for?" The young one asked the old.

"How should I know? I'm in the same place you are!"

"Yeah, jail. Hey, dad, do you think they're crowning the new king? I wonder if it's the icy-handed guy or the other one or the older man... Whichever it is, I bet he'll be a better king than you were."

The old man growled. "Don't bet your heart on it, Sully, one day I will get my revenge."

They sat there in silence for two minutes, then Sully spoke up again.

"Wow, it's brighter in the dungeon than it was anywhere in the castle when you were king."

"So?"

"I like it."

The old man growled again.

"Dad, maybe you should try to clear your throat by coughing instead of growling like that. I don't think its working."

Two more minutes past and Sully opened his mouth to speak again.

"Um..." He started.

"Sully?"

"Yes, dad?"

"Do me a favour."

"Anything, dad."

"Shut up." The old man hung his head. This was going to be a long night, if his son kept acting like a chatterbox. He could still hear the cheering from outside. "Nobody before me was a better king than I was, and nobody ever will be." He mumbled under his breath. "I will get my revenge." But high above, the happy couples were dancing and partying and having a great time, oblivious to what was going on downstairs. Not even the guard heard the old man breathe his last breath.

"Dad, dad, dad?" Sully elbowed the old man and the limp body swung on the chains. "Noooooooooooo!"

"Get... revenge..." The old man rasped before dropping his head. And that was the end of evil king Endrion.

The echoes of laughter burned the young man's heart as his father slowly slipped away to spend the rest of his days in a fiery world that he, himself had created. And the thing is, only in Dovera do fires not burn people.

"I promise you, father, I will get revenge." The young man had anger burning in his eyes and hatred spewing in his spirit.

But the thing with revenge, my friends, is that no matter how much poison you drink, the other person will never die, but it will slowly corrode your life and leave it in ruins. Sully learned that the hard way; and I hope, my friends, that you don't make the same mistake.

Epilogue: One year later

Psalm 9:10 (NKJV)
"And those who know Your name will put their trust in You; for
You, LORD, have not forsaken those who seek You."

I was lying on the bed, my bed. Our house had been rebuilt and my parents had moved back in. I had built my own home, and Dawn had joined me to make it enjoyable. I sat on my bed and wrote in a page of the notebook Bettie had given to me all those months ago. I wrote to show that behind all the heartache and sadness, everything turned out alright in the end. Everything happened just the way God wanted.

Mrs. Bejweld, who has had enough adventures for her time, has recently moved to Earth and found a man to hook up with. The man for her turned out to be our old neighbour Mr. Solater. They were married one month ago and have been living 'happily ever after' ever since as Mr. and Mrs. Solater.

Seth and Anne turned out to be a good couple after all. Anne is pregnant and they are living in Dovera, spreading the Word of the Lord. Seth is a great king and is solving many of Dovera's problems that the old king had made. He decreed all creatures' equal rights as humans in Dovera and all are living safely and happily under his reign. Anne has the hard job of decorating the castle. She decided to keep the cave carvings and there seems to be a change in them, they now know love. She put up banners and designed rooms and painted the stones in the hallways to give the place some colour. I am very proud of both of them. Anne's parents are happy in Dovera and are being treated like royalty. They are happy that their little girl is safe and are very proud of her husband and soon-to-be child. They still can't believe that they are going to be grandparents. They love the view from their balcony and are generally happy with everything about Dovera... except they are a little afraid that most people have powers, and a little afraid of the griffins that fly by their balcony, screeching loud and long. I guess it's something they'll get used to over time. They are particularly fond of the centaurs, though, and love going for long rides and walks and talking with them.

Dawn still hasn't posed the question, but he's been acting strange for two months now. I know he'll probably ask soon. I am so happy and life has gone my way. Living with Dawn is proving difficult, though; he is like any other man and won't ask for help when he doesn't know what to do. I guess it's a small price to pay for happiness, but what if it wrecks more than our air-conditioning? I'm kidding; we'll probably find a way to get through it. Oh, I love him so much. I didn't know love would be this sweet.

"Hey," I said as he barged in. I sat up in bed. Dawn was in a suit and tie, I'd better mark that in my notebook, he doesn't wear them often. "What's with the frills?" I asked, smiling. He smiled back in his crooked, boyish way and then quirked an eyebrow at me.

"Don't do that, Dawn, it makes me giggle."

"Come, I have something to ask you, M." I followed him as he led me into the living room where Mom and Dad huddled in the corner with a video tape. I shook my head and smiled. Anne and Seth were here, too, all the way from Dovera along with the new Mr. and Mrs. Solater.

I opened my mouth and gaped. The room was decorated with tinsel and streamers and balloons. The walls were shining with posters and pictures of Dawn and I in hearts. I smiled and turned to Dawn and gave him a big hug. We were all safe and out of harms way, now it was time for fun.

ᴄ❧

The night that followed was full of memories, laughing and dancing. And this time the dancing wasn't forced. We all truly enjoyed ourselves and I got to feel the little baby kicking in Anne's tummy. She was hoping for a boy, an heir for Seth to give the throne of Dovera to when he grew up. I thought a girl would be fun.

It was a joyous time. We even sang some songs that Anne and I remembered from Awana. We ended the night out on the porch watching the sunset.

"I don't know how to put this in better words than Seth did to Anne," Dawn started as we sat in the warm night air, "But Morning Star, the light of my life, will you sacrifice all to come and be my queen and lawful wedded wife?" He cocked an eyebrow in a way only Dawn could do and that melted me right then and there.

"I need to think about that." I joked, looking down at my dog, "Should I marry this man pooch?" The Bichon Shih-Tzu quirked her head at my voice,

"I don't care what you say," I told Coco, scratching behind her ears. I turned to Dawn, "There is no doubt about my answer."

"Oh? Then what is it?" I knew he was holding his breath, along with half the family hiding behind the window.

"Yes." My simple answer was all he needed to be satisfied.

"Kiss her, kiss her, KISS HER!" The rest of the family chanted as they came out from behind the door all at once, but Dawn didn't need someone to tell him. He leaned forward and kissed me softly and sweetly. Everyone cheered. Tonight wasn't the end, not at all! It was just the beginning.

"Honey, I know now you were the Morning Star that the old man said I would go on a journey with. It has been dangerous, but well worth it. Well, I guess you'll have to settle with being Morning Starlight now, but in my heart you will always be my Morning Star."

I smiled at him, "I wouldn't have it any other way." And he kissed me again while the family started to dance to upbeat, happy music.

Looking back, I really wouldn't have had it any other way.

The End...

Reviews:

"A well written book with amazingly spectacular imagery."
--- Christopher (Brother)

"Imagination plus belief plus faith plus perseverance plus love plus Jesus yields thoughts and actions and stories which will change the world for the better. Well done."
--- With love, from Dad.

"Absolutely Awesome Story! I've watched you work long and hard by the hour on the computer. jotting down thoughts for your "story" in your notebook at any time and any place and adding thoughts and situations you have pulled from real life. This truly is a work of art and a labour of love that you have poured your heart and soul into as you weave the Truth of God's love throughout every chapter. I'm so very proud of you."
--- I Love you, Mom.

"Wow! G. Davidson has created a masterpiece! Very imaginative!"
--- Mrs. Kuzma (Gr. 8 Humanities teacher)

"Creative, wonderful and authentic! "
--- Breanne (Best friend)

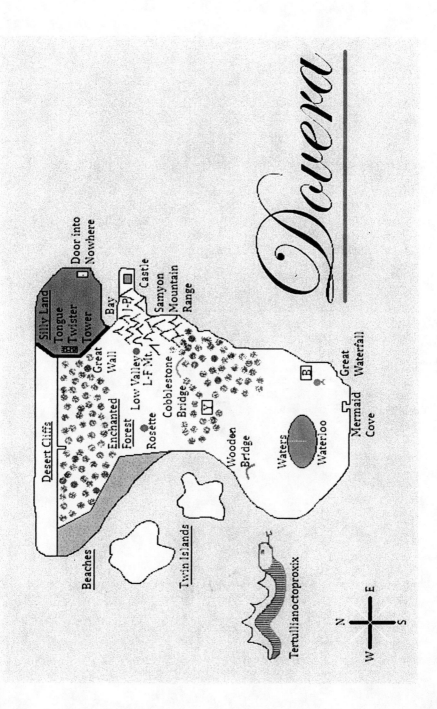

LaVergne, TN USA
21 January 2010
170803LV00001B/32/P